TORN

Suzanne Featherstonehaugh

Copyright © 2023
Suzanne Featherstonehaugh
All rights reserved

ABOUT THE AUTHOR

Suzanne Featherstonehaugh was born in Shropshire, in 1945. A mother of three lovely children and a grandmother, she has always been creative from a very early age, loves to paint, cook and dance.

Torn is based on fact and fiction. It was written in 2004 during a traumatic time in Suzanne's life. They do say there is one book in all of us. This is Suzanne's

Suzanne Featherstonehaugh
June 2023

ACKNOWLEDGEMENTS

Special thanks go to my beloved children, Julian, Melanie and James, and my son-in-law, Russ, for assisting with the technicalities. Also, special love goes to the 'Girl Fridays' (they know who they are). Deepest thanks are due to Beverly and Brian for their patience and clarity – they finally made it possible to publish this book

CREDITS

Initial proofreading and editing:
Francesca Ridley

Final proofreading:
Beverly Lambert

Assistance in publishing this book:
Brian Huggett

Cover design:
Francesca Ridley

PREFACE

In 2004, I wrote a book whilst I was going through a traumatic time in my personal life. It started out as a short story for a competition, but I had so much to say that it ended up as a novella. The female lead is not me, though. She has everything that I had lost and, whilst I adored her, I was deeply jealous of her, too.

My manuscript gathered dust for nearly twenty years until I met a group of ladies and, when I came to know them well, I mentioned my book. Over the next few months, we read parts of the story together and laughed till we cried and cried till we laughed. We knew it simply had to be published, but we did not know how. That is when friends of friends stepped in and, gradually, *Torn* became a reality.

CHAPTER 1

"Good morning. Lawson & Partners. How may I help you?"

"Hello, good morning. Mrs Darling here. Please may I speak to Mr Lawson?"

There was silence.

"Are you family, or a friend of the family?"

"We are good friends of the family," Jennifer replied, hesitatingly.

There was more silence. The receptionist spoke with a quiver in her voice.

"I am very sorry to be the conveyer of such sad news, but Mr Lawson was fatally injured last Friday evening on his way home from the office." Jennifer hesitated. She was horrified at the news she was hearing. This couldn't be true! She could feel the tears welling up inside. There was more silence.

"Mrs Darling, are you still there?"

"Yes, I'm still here," said Jennifer, in shock.

"His funeral is on Friday morning at their village church. He is to be cremated afterwards, which will be a private ceremony for the family only."

"Oh." Jennifer could hardly believe the words she was hearing. Trying to hold back the tears, she put her hand over the mouthpiece, but tears started to stream down her face.

"Mrs Darling, are you still there?"

"Yes," she said with a shudder. "Yes … I'm still here. I'll discuss it with my husband. Goodbye." Jennifer put the receiver back…ping. The ping of the phone took her right back to the announcement at the airport where they had first seen each other.

"Attention! Will all passengers for London Heathrow now embark at Gate 22."

Jennifer is in her fifties, a natural blonde and young for her age. She is bubbly and enjoys life. As she was listening out for the announcement of her flight back home, she noticed a rather handsome gentleman standing to her right: well-dressed, a smart suit. Similar age, she thought. He walked past and smiled - a lovely smile, she thought.

"He looks dishy, Mummy," said Lydia. "Wouldn't it be lovely if he was on your flight?" she teased.

"Oh, Lydia!"

"I just thought to accompany you on your journey, that's all!"

Jennifer's mind, having wandered for a moment, now returned to hear Gate 22 announced. She was full of emotion, saying goodbye to Lydia - and especially to the newest member of their family, darling little Noah.

"Oh, that's my flight!"

"Mummy, you'll be fine," Lydia reassured her. "You have plenty of time."

"You know me and flying - especially landing."

"Daddy will be there to meet you."

"No, your father said he was going to meet the train at Hereford station when I get in tomorrow afternoon. Having a night flight means I'll arrive refreshed tomorrow. Well, my darling, thank you for a lovely time; I also really enjoyed spending time with our new little special member of the family - although you know your father's and my feelings about the name Noah: we must buy him an ark for his christening present!"

"Oh, Mummy, you're so horrid."

"I'm only teasing, Lydia! We're delighted that Noah Jack Farrington is to be christened where we were married and where you were also christened and married. I'll find some dates in June. Lots of love to all of you, my darlings. I must go now so I can find a seat in the departure lounge and gather my thoughts before I have to board." She smiled warmly at her daughter. "I'll phone in a couple of days, once I've recovered, with June dates for the christening."

Jennifer gave Lydia more hugs and kisses and gave an extra cuddle to Noah. As she was hurrying towards check-in, she turned and gave a final wave and blew a kiss.

"Bye, Mummy - love you," Lydia waved back.

"Will all passengers for London Heathrow now embark at Gate 22."

CHAPTER 2

Simon, a lawyer returning from a business trip in Kuwait, was listening out for the announcement of his flight to Heathrow. "Thank you for driving me to the airport, Cliff."

"I couldn't let you get a taxi. That's what friends are for."

"Well, it was very kind of you; I know how busy you are. I'll send the signed documents as soon as possible - certainly after the weekend."

"Thanks, Simon. See you in six weeks." Cliff shook Simon by the hand. "I always look forward to your visits. Enjoy your flight."

"Yes, I always enjoy coming here – it's both work and pleasure. Give my love to Samantha. Cheerio!"

He walked towards the check-in counter and, as he approached the desk, he saw a family saying their farewells. The mother had obviously been visiting them. He smiled and nodded his head as he made his way to check-in. He put his battered old suitcase on the scales. The hostess was putting on a label, looking at Simon and then the case, and was clearly thinking that his battered case did not quite suit a gentleman of this calibre. Simon noticed her puzzled look. "A twenty-first present from an ancient aunt – I've never had the heart to throw it away. I think it will be with me till my grave."

She smiled. "You have plenty of time, Mr Lawson," she said, returning his ticket and passport to him.

"Thank you," he smiled in return.

Simon walked towards the departure lounge, entering immigration and went through the automatic doors. It was quite airy after all that heat of the last few weeks. I could do with a gin and tonic, he thought, glancing at his watch. He went over to the kiosk.

"The Times, please," he requested and paid for it. "Thank you." He was looking forward to catching up on what had been happening in the UK and was thinking he would sit and read his paper and lose himself whilst waiting for his flight. There were people looking worried. There are some who are afraid of flying; airports are scary places, he thought. Ah, here is a seat. He put his briefcase down by the side of the seat, sat down and opened his newspaper. Two weeks spent in Kuwait and there had been no time to pick up a paper, or to socialise. If only Sylvia would come, just once; we could have so much fun, but she doesn't like flying or holidaying in the sun.

He glanced down the line whilst he was opening his paper, his mind occupied with thoughts of what he was going to do this weekend: some gardening, walk the dogs. Sylvia will probably do her own thing with her friends. Looking up from his thoughts, not concentrating on his paper, the lady that he had seen earlier walked past and sat opposite him. She looked very smart. She was wearing a rather nice white shirt and beige skirt and was carrying her jacket. Not the usual lady traveller. This lady had lovely legs. He was used to seeing his wife wearing jeans or jogging pants. She rarely wore pretty shoes like those. I must stop peeping around my paper. She might become suspicious. She's very nice and seemed to have a lovely family saying goodbye to her in the airport foyer.

Jennifer Darling smiled at the gentleman as she sat opposite him, hoping that he did not think her too forward. She always smiles at everybody. He smiled back, nodded his head and went back to his paper. He is rather dishy. Perhaps Lydia's observation earlier was correct. Very smart nice suit, shiny shoes, slim. I think quite tall. Returning from a business trip, thought Jennifer.

Darling Peter, oh, darling Peter! Round, rotund, built like a Hereford bull, but, oh, so lovely, so sweet and considerate. A girl could not wish for a kinder husband. I just wish he could smarten himself up occasionally. He always looks as though he has thrown his clothes on. As Mummy said: he looks like he has just got out of bed. Well, I'm a farmer's wife - Mrs Peter Darling, a farmer's wife. I'll see him tomorrow, when I'll be greeted by one of his usual bear-hugging hugs. Can't wait to see my lovely shiny black horse! I hope she hasn't missed me too much. And Chi Chi, my wonderful spaniel with floppy ears and lovely big brown eyes. I love them both so much! Jennifer was startled as she heard the announcement, listening particularly because of her fear of getting on the wrong plane. Yes, that's my flight.

"Will all first-class passengers please now board." Jennifer rose from her seat and smiled at the gentleman opposite her. Obviously, he's not on my flight – oh, dash! Quite funny having these feelings. She remembered the time when she was a teenager and had a crush on Michael Heath. She walked towards the boarding gate. Here we go, she thought. Lots of people hustling around Gate 22. Yes, there it is! I've arrived. At least I'll be on the right flight.

CHAPTER 3

The stewardess held her hand out to take Jennifer's boarding pass. She's friendly, thought Jennifer. What a pity that chap who was opposite me in the departure lounge isn't on my flight. I wish I'd had time to go to the bar and relax with a gin and tonic. Oh, well! I can have one on the plane. The stewardess greeted her with a cheery smile.

"Good evening and welcome."

"Good evening. May I sit by a window?" asked Jennifer.

"There's plenty of room, so you can choose where you would like to sit."

"Thank you," Jennifer replied with a smile and moved down the plane until she found a suitable window seat. "I'll sit here. Thank you very much."

"Would you like me to put your jacket in the overhead luggage space?"

"No, thank you. I always think it's a little chilly when we get airborne and I may pop it around my shoulders."

"We have blankets and pillows in the seat in front of you, Mrs Darling. Just ring if you want anything."

"Thank you." Jennifer sat down to prepare herself for the flight. She looked around at all the people busily finding their seats and picked up her bag. At least I have a good book, if I get bored, and I can always have a sleep.

Simon watched as the lady walked away. She smiled. A lovely lady. Wondering what long journey she will be taking tonight, he stood up and picked up his briefcase, thinking about a few things that he could catch up with on the plane. I'll find a comfortable seat - plenty of room in first-class - spread myself out, order an enormous G and T, look at the menu. I hope there is seafood. I'll then settle down and enjoy the weekend before going into the office on Monday morning. His mind had been wandering so much that Gate 22 was now right in front of him. He handed his boarding pass to the stewardess and approached the plane.

"Good evening, Mr Lawson. Very nice to see you again."

"I know," said Simon. "We must stop meeting like this!" He laughed.

"I will be around with the drinks once we're airborne."

Simon boarded the plane and popped his head into the compartment. There, sitting by the window, was the attractive lady who had sat opposite him earlier. Jennifer was trying to relax and had her nose in her book, having started to read it just a few days ago. She couldn't wait to find out if the lead female character was going to leave her husband. She hadn't noticed that Simon had entered the plane. Simon walked down the aisle and stopped by Jennifer's seat. "Would you have any objection if I sit next to you?"

Jennifer smiled. "No, I don't have any objection," she replied, secretly thinking it would be rather nice to spend the journey home with an extremely handsome companion. Lydia did say it would be lovely if he was on my flight and here he is, sitting next to me! I feel warm and safe. I must phone Lydia tomorrow. She'll be tickled pink.

Simon opened the overhead luggage space, put his briefcase inside, closed the hatch and sat down, putting his newspaper on his lap. He smiled at her, picked up his paper and started to peruse the front page. The fragrance of her perfume stirred him. He folded his paper and put it in the pocket in the seat in front of him. She was very attractive. I don't think that I'll be doing any work this evening. How funny that, out of all those people at the airport, she's on my flight, he thought.

"I think that, in view of the fact we're going to spend the journey home together, I will introduce myself. My name is Simon Lawson." He handed the drinks' menu to Jennifer. "I'm married with two sons and live in Sussex." He then gestured to

Jennifer to introduce herself.

"I'm Jennifer Darling, married with one daughter. I have just been visiting her and her husband and baby in Kuwait."

"I saw you in the airport foyer," said Simon. "You looked like a lovely family. Your husband doesn't come with you?" He noticed the rings on her wedding finger.

"No, we have a farm in Herefordshire. Although we have farmhands, my husband likes to keep an eye on the animals and things. He's not keen on travelling very far – just to the pub and the golf course."

They start chatting, words coming very easily.

"When we're airborne, I think it would be rather nice if we went up to the bar and spent part of the journey home relaxing and enjoying each other's company," Simon suggested.

"I would like that very much. What a lovely idea!" replied Jennifer.

The stewardess demonstrated the usual safety procedures and announced that they were about to taxi down the runway. "I'm a little nervous of flying," Jennifer said, "especially landing. I'm always very happy when we're above the clouds and they ask you if you'd like a drink. I always say 'yes, please - a large G and T'," she laughed. I'm going to enjoy this journey home, she thought.

Simon also had similar thoughts. The plane started to gather speed down the runway. Simon could see that Jennifer was a little apprehensive and took hold of her right hand and held it gently, but firmly. Jennifer turned and smiled. The plane climbed up and up and still Simon had hold of her hand. As the plane was levelling, Simon said, "We can have that drink now."

The stewardess approached Simon and Jennifer. "May I get you some drinks now?" Simon gave her their drinks' order.

"Two large G and Ts, please."

"We'll be serving supper soon for those passengers who want to sleep. When I bring your drinks, perhaps you would like to order your food?" she said, handing Simon a menu. She then turned away, leaving Jennifer and Simon to ponder the choices.

"Now, what do I fancy?" Jennifer mused, turning to Simon, who was deep into the choice.

"Would you like seafood?" he asked, as she nodded and smiled.

"I don't want to sleep, do you?" asked Simon.

"No," replied Jennifer. "I am having far too much fun. We can have our drinks and supper and then go to the bar and let some of these people catch some shut-eye." The stewardess brought their drinks and some nibbles and Simon ordered the meals. They sat back in their seats and enjoyed sipping their gins and tonic.

"Do you visit your family in Kuwait very often?"

"My first time was two years ago. I was missing Lydia, so my husband, Peter, suggested that I come out to see her," Jennifer explained. "They usually come home to the UK every three months, except when she was pregnant, when Michael would not let her fly. So, this visit has been particularly special - saying hello to the newest member of our family and being with my darling daughter, watching her being a mother."

"What's the name of the baby?"

"Don't laugh. Peter and I have had mixed feelings and great deliberations about his name. It's Noah Jack. We like the name Jack." Simon smiled, noticing her misgivings about the name. "That's enough chit chat about me for the time being," said Jennifer. "Tell me something about you. I'd love to hear." She was feeling very relaxed in this sexy man's company.

"My wife is Sylvia. We married young and have two sons. One is a solicitor, like me, and works in my brother's and my practice. We're going to make him a partner this year - we will announce it at our company dinner. Jack is a super guy, as is Freddie, who is a GP. Jack isn't married, but Freddie is. We don't have the patter of little feet yet - we think that they both enjoy their lives and their homes too much." He smiled at her. "I don't think Sylvia minds one way or the other. She always says that she's too young to be a grandmother… If I may say so, I think you look far too young to be one." Jennifer blushed slightly.

CHAPTER 4

The suppers they had chosen earlier, when the stewardess collected their empty glasses, had arrived and, with them, a bottle of chilled wine in a cooler, along with two crystal glasses. "I didn't know we were having wine with our supper," said Jennifer as she pointed to the wine.

They had both ordered fruits de mer. Simon filled Jennifer's glass and then his own. Raising his glass towards hers, he said, "My dear, we have an eight-hour journey in front of us and, when we land at Heathrow, we will part forever. I raise my glass to a lovely lady."

"Thank you! And I raise my glass to a perfect gentleman."

They were getting on famously, thought Simon. What a charming lady to spend the eight hours with. As he raised some lobster towards his lips, Jennifer watched this action and thought what lovely lips he had. Good enough to kiss. Oh, my goodness! I haven't had thoughts like this for years!

"We couldn't have ordered a nicer supper," Simon commented.

"I love fish," Jennifer answered. "If I was told tomorrow that not another morsel of meat may pass my lips for the rest of my life, I just couldn't care less. Ooh, I think the wine is going a little bit to my head!"

"No," said Simon, "we're just relaxing and enjoying each other's company."

Indeed we are, thought Jennifer.

"I love Peter very much, but we live quite separate lives. Well, I don't mean separate lives. We're relaxed with each other, no flashing lights," she confided to Simon. "Rather like a pair of comfortable slippers by the fire."

They had both now finished their delicious supper and Simon was enjoying listening to Jennifer's voice. He smiled. "I think I know what you mean. You don't have to explain." He was enjoying the freeness of their conversation. "I feel as though I've known you all my life - or perhaps we met in a previous life."

"Oh, do you really feel like that?" asked Jennifer, feeling slightly tipsy.

"I do. I just wish it didn't have to end tomorrow when we say goodbye."

Simon took her hand. They were very quiet as some of the overhead lights were going out around them. "If we stay in our seats, I agree that we will nod off, so shall we go up to the cocktail bar?" Simon gestured to Jennifer to go up the stairs first. As she climbed the spiral staircase, Simon followed, studying her shapely legs. He spotted a table. "Let's sit over there." They sat down. "Should we continue with wine, or would you like something different?"

"Champagne, please!" replied Jennifer, without hesitation. "Please may we have champagne?" Simon smiled.

"I have heard of the mile high club, but I don't think it has anything to do with drinking!" he said. He got up from his seat, leant forward and gave Jennifer a kiss on her cheek. "Champagne, it is. Coming right up. What the lady orders, the lady gets."

Jennifer was rather pleased that he had gone to the bar to order champagne, as it gave her an opportunity to observe this very attractive man, who had just given her a gentle kiss. Wait until I tell Lydia! She just won't believe it – though, neither do I! What's happening to me? I haven't had these feelings for a very long time!

Simon was wearing a very smart grey suit and blue shirt. She had noticed his amusing tie earlier: sandy camels on a royal blue silk background. He turned to Jennifer. "Moët or Taittinger?" he asked.

"I'll let you choose," replied Jennifer, hardly believing the attention she was receiving. She glanced down at her shoes and tapped her toes together. Simon returned with the champagne and placed it on the table.

"I do like your shoes. I noticed them in the departure lounge…attached to a lovely pair of legs!"

"I didn't think that you'd noticed me."

"Indeed I did - especially your love." He leaned forward and stroked her leg. "Oh, sorry," he said. "I'm just getting a little bit carried away!" He poured Jennifer's champagne and handed the glass to her. "To us," he said and smiled. They were sitting quite close to each other. He put his glass on the table and then took Jennifer's glass from her hand and placed it next to his. He held her hands and looked directly into her eyes.

CHAPTER 5

"I'm very attracted to you – ever since your first lovely smile at the airport. And we really enjoy each other's company." Simon leant in a little closer to Jennifer. "Am I right? Do you feel the same?"

"Yes, I do," said Jennifer, squeezing his hand. She was enjoying his approach as he looked into her blue eyes.

Simon thought that, with what he was about to say, she would either slap him across the face or, hopefully, kiss him on his cheek.

"Jennifer, I would very much like to spend some more time with you. I'm so pleased I've met you and, if you think that the suggestion I am about to make to you is absolutely out of the question …," he paused, "… then, as soon as I've finished, I want you to leave your seat - and me sitting here - and go back downstairs. I'll ask for another seat and the whole situation and embarrassment on my part will be at an end." He moved closer. "As I said, we will be landing soon, never to see each other again, but it seems we both feel the same about each other." He took a deep breath. "I would also like to say that I don't make a habit of picking up attractive ladies at airports." He smiled at her. "And I haven't felt this attracted to anyone for a very long time."

Jennifer braced herself, wondering what on earth he was going to say.

"When we land, let's spend the day together." He squeezed Jennifer's hand. "And possibly the evening?"

"Oh, I would love that!" whispered Jennifer, kissing him on the cheek. Delighted, Simon kissed her gently on her lips.

"I'm incredibly attracted to you. It might be the freeness, no complications between us...or far too much champagne! If you don't go home until tomorrow, would that cause any problems with your husband?"

"No, I'll phone him when we land. He isn't picking me up at the airport. I'm going home by train and he's collecting me from the station late afternoon. What about your commitments?" asked Jennifer.

"I'm fairly flexible. We have a flat in town that I use when I work late or need to stay in town. I'll tell Sylvia that I'm staying there tonight, as I'm unexpectedly having supper with clients this evening."

Three days ago, thought Jennifer…just three days ago. I've been longing to hear his voice again. Peter disturbed her thoughts.

"Are you all right, darling? You look so sad."

"Yes, I was just thinking about Lydia and Noah and that I was with them this time last week. I miss her so much. I hate her being so far away."

"Cheer up. We'll see them soon. Think about organising the christening. You'll enjoy that." He gave her his handkerchief to wipe her eyes.

"Thank you." She dabbed at her tears and returned it to him.

"There's a quiz at the pub tonight and you can tell all our friends about your trip to Kuwait and show off the photographs of Noah." Peter was heading for the door. "I won't be back for lunch, chicken." The door banged as he slammed it.

Friday. Only Friday, she thought, and her mind drifted back to that wonderful night.

"We'll make our respective phone calls when we land," said Simon.

"It's rather exciting!" giggled Jennifer.

Neither of them had noticed the other people in the bar, but they both suddenly realised they were becoming the centre of attention.

"I bet they think that we're…"

Jennifer put two fingers on his lips. "Shh," she said. "We both know what they're thinking. Should we let them have something else to think about?" Simon put his arms around her, held her tightly and kissed her with feeling on her lips. They both broke away laughing and got up from the table and made their way back to their seats.

"We will be landing shortly. Will all passengers please return to their seats and fasten their seat belts," the speaker crackled.

As Simon was fastening his seat belt, he turned to Jennifer and said, "We haven't spent very much time here, have we?" She smiled. The plane started to descend and Simon gently held her hand.

"We're coming back down to earth. It's not too late to change your mind."

"I'm not going to change my mind," said Jennifer, as she sat back in her seat, anticipating the apprehension she usually felt when landing, but there was none. She felt safe and warm and extremely happy. Is this really happening to me? she thought.

The plane landed smoothly and taxied along the runway.

"Will all passengers please remain in their seats until the plane is at a standstill."

"London," Simon said. "Six-thirty in the morning." He opened the overhead locker and retrieved Jennifer's hand luggage. He removed his bag and took Jennifer's small hand case. They started to disembark, saying their farewells to the aircrew on the way out. Once outside the plane, they could feel the chill in the air in comparison to Kuwait.

Simon placed Jennifer's jacket around her shoulders, picked up both their cases and they started to walk towards customs.

"Jennifer, darling."

"Yes, Simon, darling."

"Let's do all the red tape and get our phone calls out of the way."

They walked through immigration together.

"Well, that's over with. We need a trolley!" Simon went and found one and came back to Jennifer.

"I was just thinking: if you hadn't been here, I would have had to do this all by myself," mused Jennifer.

"You poor thing…a damsel in distress!"

"My father used to call me Butterfly." Simon looked at her, puzzled. "Damsel Butterfly." They both giggled.

The luggage carousel started to whirr. "Here come our bags." The people on the flight, whom they had hardly noticed, stood around, eagerly trying to identify their cases.

"That's mine," said Simon, as a battered old leather suitcase came rumbling up the ramp. "It was a present from my old aunt many years ago. I never thought about the need to replace it." Jennifer, for the first time, saw an outline of his bottom as he leaned over to pick up the case. She felt all warm and overcome. I must be having a hot flush, she thought, knowing full well the effect this man was beginning to have on her.

"Just one case?" asked Jennifer.

"Yes, I like to travel light. I bet you've got dozens of suitcases. An outfit for various functions of the day," he teased.

"Well, not quite that many," she smiled, knowing that she would not have missed this encounter for the world.

"Those are mine, the red ones!" she pointed. "All three in a row…no, there's one more!" A very large, red suitcase came rumbling around on the carousel. Simon lifted the heavy case off.

"What have you got in here, Jennifer, darling? The Kuwaiti crown jewels?"

"Yes, don't tell everyone!" They both laughed.

CHAPTER 6

Simon loaded up the trolley and they made their way, hand in hand, through customs and on towards the phone booths.

"Actually, I'd like to freshen up first," said Jennifer, eyeing the ladies' toilets. I'm absolutely dying to spend a penny, she thought. As they started to move apart, Simon said, as he gently pulled Jennifer close to him again, "Do you realise that this will be the first time we will have spent time apart since we met?"

"I know! But I'm dying to spend a penny," whispered Jennifer, reluctantly pulling herself away. He kissed her and she went through the door.

She looked in the mirror, freshened up her face and lips, sprayed a little perfume on her hair, dried her hands and paused to look in the mirror once more. What's happening to me? She couldn't wait to get back to Simon and returned feeling refreshed. Simon was there, gazing intently at her.

"Did you think I might run away?" asked Jennifer. "Now, I've been thinking about what to say to Peter and I've decided to tell him that I'm very tired after my journey and have decided to take the afternoon train tomorrow - the same time as today, but tomorrow. It's his birthday soon and, before I left, he hinted that he would like a new fishing rod. So, I'll say that I'm going to book into a hotel and get up early to do some shopping and bits and pieces for his sixtieth birthday and tell him that I'm looking forward to seeing him tomorrow."

"Well, you've convinced me! I almost believe you myself," smiled Simon.

"What will your explanation be?"

"So, mine is less complicated than that. I'll phone the office and ask my secretary to phone home and explain that, after my return and subsequent visit to the office, I had to visit one of our clients and that I would probably be dining with those particular clients, but perhaps phone her this evening."

"Much more logical than mine," she nodded. "Peter will think I've grown up. He knows how much I hate being on my own and making decisions, so he'll be very proud of me!"

Simon put his arm around Jennifer's waist and asked, "You are all right about this, aren't you? You haven't changed your mind?"

"No, don't be silly," she reassured him and kissed him gently on the cheek. He opened the telephone booth door for Jennifer and she stepped in.

"I'll turn around so that I don't put you off." He gave her arm a gentle squeeze as she entered the kiosk. She smiled and closed the door after her. Simon watched her dial and, when she started to speak, he turned his back to her for what seemed an age. He watched people rushing past on various journeys of their lives. The door eventually opened and Simon turned around.

"Yes, that's fine. Peter thought it quite sensible and even told me the particular fishing rod he would like for his birthday. He said, if I was too tired this evening, he would understand if I don't phone."

Simon smiled. "You don't feel guilty, do you?"

"No, I should…but I don't," replied Jennifer.

Simon then entered the kiosk and made his phone call.

Phone calls having been made, they then set off, Simon pushing the trolley full of their luggage. "We need a taxi and then a hotel. I think it would be rather nice for our time together to be at The Ritz or The Savoy." Jennifer wasn't going to argue with that. "Here's the taxi queue. Let's wait here." He turned to Jennifer. "So, which will it be?"

"The Ritz!" said Jennifer and linked her arm through his.

"The Ritz it is!"

"I hope we can book in," said Jennifer.

"If not, we'll find somewhere else," replied Simon. He gave her hand a little stroke and looked into her eyes. It made Jennifer go all gooey. He smiled. "I thought that I would be going to my office, organising things to do next week and, then, I see this lovely lady at the airport, looking stunning in her smart clothes and with those fantastic legs…the shoes with little heels and carrying your jacket … and your fantastic legs!"

"You've already mentioned my legs," laughed Jennifer, as Simon smiled.

"And I will keep on saying it...fantastic legs!"

It was now their turn for the taxi. Simon put the luggage in the boot with the help of the taxi driver. "What have you got in here, guv?"

"The Kuwaiti crown jewels," replied Simon.

"Don't listen to him!" said Jennifer, while scowling at Simon. They both laughed and settled down in the back of the taxi.

"You had a good flight?" the driver asked, being a friendly kind of chap.

"We did. We had a memorable flight." Simon and Jennifer looked into each other's eyes.

"Where to, sir?"

"The Ritz, please," said Simon. "We're a bit tired now, so my wife and I are going to check into The Ritz before we go home to Cardiff tomorrow." Simon gave her hand a squeeze, really wanting to kiss her lips, but he kissed her cheek and nuzzled his nose into her ear. Jennifer enjoyed the moment.

"Oh, I love being in a proper taxi, travelling around London, watching people from all over the world visiting this fantastic city." Simon loved her enthusiasm. She was so adorable, he thought. He put his arm around her.

"Here we are," the driver announced, as the taxi stopped outside The Ritz. Simon paid the taxi driver and gave him a tip.

"Enjoy your time here, sir."

"What a nice taxi driver," said Jennifer. "He probably thought you were going to give him a huge tip." Simon tapped Jennifer's bottom.

"Now, what's our name? Who do we register as? Oh! There's the porter. He can help me carry our luggage to reception and then we can choose a surname together," said Simon.

Jennifer made her way towards the entrance. As she looked up at this lovely hotel, she pondered on how, at this time yesterday, when she was packing her case, she thought she would be returning to her normal life – yet, she was here!

Simon returned. "I managed to grab the porter and he's taken our luggage to the desk. So, what should we call ourselves? Not Mr and Mrs Smith - that's far too obvious!" They were standing next to two large bay trees.

"How about Mr and Mrs Baytree?" Jennifer laughed.

"Mr and Mrs Green sounds a little more plausible," smiled Simon. They walked into the foyer and Simon found Jennifer a seat. "Would you like some coffee? I can ask someone to bring us some while I go and check in… Please may my wife and I have a pot of coffee?"

CHAPTER 7

That coffee was so thoughtful. Jennifer reluctantly left the memories.

She was feeling drained and cold with shock. She walked into the kitchen, put the kettle on and picked up Chi Chi, her spaniel. "I've been neglecting you. I'm so sorry." She hugged her, gaining just a touch of comfort from her little warm body. She put some food into Chi Chi's bowl and placed it by the Rayburn cooker. "There you are, my darling. It's nice and warm by the fire."

Jennifer made her cup of coffee and sat on the chair nearest the fire. Chi Chi had finished her food, so Jennifer picked her up again. She was sipping her mug of coffee, whilst Chi Chi was on her lap, nuzzling her comforting nose into Jennifer's arm. The tears started to stream down her face. Why, oh, why? We had such a lovely time together, finding one another, loving one another. I feel so empty. I know that I shouldn't. His poor family! What hell they must be going through! She put her coffee back onto the table and stroked Chi Chi. She stared into her coffee on the table.

"Your coffee, Madam."
"Thank you."

"Would you like me to pour it for you, Madam?"

"No, thank you. I'll wait for my husband." It almost sounded real. She glanced over to reception and Simon was checking them in for a night of love, she hoped. She decided she couldn't wait for the coffee, so poured herself a lovely hot cup, leaned back in her chair and took a delicious sip.

Several minutes later, Simon came over. "All done. We're booked into room twenty-four. Have you finished your coffee, darling?"

"Yes." Jennifer rose from her seat. "What about your coffee?"

"I'll order another pot from our room." Simon pointed towards the lift. They were greeted by the porter.

"This way, Madam."

They entered the lift and Simon put his arm around Jennifer's waist. He smiled at her. Those eyes, thought Jennifer. He only has to smile and I'm totally gone.

"This is your floor, sir," the porter said, directing them down the corridor. They found door twenty-four. Simon squeezed Jennifer's hand as the porter put the key into the lock and entered, pushing the trolley. 'Mr and Mrs Green' followed.

"Thank you for your help," said Simon, as the porter left and closed the door.

"Wow! Isn't this fantastic? Aren't we lucky? It's

so beautiful!" Jennifer rushed into the bathroom. "Look, Simon!" He followed her. "Look at this lovely bath! What a super room!"

"We can pretend that we're lovers in April in Paris."

"But I don't want to pretend," replied Jennifer. "London is wonderful - just as romantic."

"We'll see," said Simon with a smile.

"What was all that nonsense in the taxi? Cardiff, indeed!"

"I thought it was pretty good, coming just off the top of my head," Simon replied with mock indignance.

"Completely off our heads, deceiving our loved ones like this!" she said, peeping around the door.

"You can always change your mind," suggested Simon.

"No," said Jennifer. "I'm enjoying it just as it is." She leaned over and started to run her bath. She then walked towards the door, blew Simon a kiss and closed the door.

Simon, meanwhile, unlatched his old case and took out appropriate casual clothes for April: khaki trousers, red striped shirt and navy sweater. He also took out his sports jacket, not too sure whether to wear it or the sweater. He then spotted his pyjamas and smiled to himself, thinking that he wouldn't need those tonight. He was feeling extremely relaxed.

A while later, the bathroom door opened and Jennifer appeared, wrapped in a towel with a turban on her head. Seeing her looking so sexy made Simon's heart jump. He was trying to control his feelings.

"Your turn now," announced Jennifer. "Would you like me to put some smellies and bubbles into your bath?"

"Yes, please, darling. Mrs Green."

"All right! I'll do it for you, because you answered so nicely." She touched his chin softly with her fingers. He grabbed her pretty hand. He had not been touched so gently for a long time. He kissed her fingers. Jennifer poured the bubble bath into the flowing water. "It's all yours."

"Thank you."

He pulled her towards him and her towel fell to the floor. He held her tight and kissed her neck.

"You smell wonderful." His hand touched her breast.

"Aah, ah! Not just yet - perhaps later. Have your bath." She picked up her towel and wrapped it around her body, looking at him all the time.

"You're teasing me!" he said.

"I'll be waiting in the next room." She closed the door behind her. She could hear that Simon was enjoying his bath. He started to sing. "I'm forever blowing bubbles, pretty bubbles in the air..."

"You're not in tune!" called out Jennifer.

"I am! You should come in here and I can show you!"

Jennifer giggled, sat down at the dressing table, removed her turban and smoothed her hair with her brush. Her pretty underwear was laid out on the bed. She removed her towel and started to put on her panties and her bra. She left the suspender belt on the bed.

"Hope you're not getting dressed!" called Simon from the bathroom.

"Yes, I'm fully dressed," was her reply through the door.

The bathroom door opened. "I thought you said that you were dressed! I expected to come in here and see you standing there with your coat on and all I see is a vision of loveliness in lace and silk. What is a poor chap to do but take advantage of this lovely lady?" Simon had come out of the bathroom totally naked. Jennifer looked at him, not hung like a bull, but taut and magnificent, an Adonis. He was hers until tomorrow.

CHAPTER 8

He came towards her. Her tummy had butterflies. Their bodies touched. He kissed her fully and with so much passion that she could feel herself gently falling under his wonderful spell. Her lips tingled with excitement as his tongue gently played with hers. She could feel him stirring. Oh, yes, Jennifer thought. Take me! Her body was responding to his. That did not happen very often nowadays. He withdrew from her lips and kissed her shoulder. He put his hands around her back, removed her bra and touched her upright nipples with his fingers. His head went down and he gently slipped her nipple into his warm mouth. Jennifer felt as though her legs were going to give way. His tongue played with her nipple. Oh, never stop! Oh,yes, please! Take me to that bed, deflower me, take me to heights I have only heard about!

Simon moved across and did the same to her other nipple, his free hand gently caressing the nipple that he had already sent skywards. She felt dizzy with so much desire. She slowly lowered her hand to his eager penis and gently touched it. He gently guided her towards the bed and slowly removed her panties. By now, Jennifer could not have cared less if he had ripped them off. He peeled them off and touched her clitoris very gently. She was very responsive. Simon lay her on the bed and reclined beside her. He kissed her and slowly moved down her body, saying hello to her attentive breasts on the way. He gently touched her clitoris and moved his fingers towards her moist vagina. He kissed her nipples and moved down further as he brushed her clitoris with his tongue and took it into his mouth. Wow, golly, oh, don't ever stop! Her body became really warm. I'm having another of those hot flushes, she thought, as his lips closed. Please, just make love to me, thought Jennifer as she climaxed and felt so wonderful, desirable and loved. He released his grip on her clitoris and moved up her body. She could feel that he was ready for their encounter. He rose and lowered himself between her inviting legs, then entered her. Oh, oh, what a lovely feeling! Jennifer's eyes were closed. She put her arms around him and groped that wonderful bottom she had seen earlier at the luggage terminal. He moved gently in and out of her, smelling her aroma and drinking in her sighs. He started moving a little faster, exciting Jennifer even more. She held him tight. She could feel him deep inside her. Her sighs grew louder and then they both climaxed together like a magnificent concerto. Is this what true love really is? thought Jennifer, as tears started to stream down her face.

The memory of those tears of love! Not like the tears she has now for the loss of something she did not own. Chi Chi licked her tears. The phone was ringing. She put Chi Chi down on the floor and walked towards the phone. Wiping her cheeks with a rather damp hand, she picked up the receiver. "Hello," she said in a soft voice.

"Jennifer? It's Carol. You sound awful. Are you all right?"

"Oh, yes. It's an emotional time with the baby and Lydia."

"Is she okay?"

"Yes, yes. I think I must still be jet-lagged."

"Peter saw Charles and he said that you'd stayed overnight in The Ritz, you lucky thing! Anyway, the reason I'm phoning is to ask whether we're all going to have supper in the pub this evening?"

"Yes, yes," said Jennifer. "Can you book a table, please, Carol?"

"Of course! I'm looking forward to hearing all the news about Noah. I hope you feel better by this evening."

"If I don't, Peter can bring along the photographs."

"I hope you do feel better. I'm looking forward to seeing you and hearing about your night in London. Did a lovely chap persuade you to stay overnight?" she enquired, cheekily.

"I should be so lucky!" replied Jennifer with a pang of guilt.

"Looking forward to seeing you this evening," Carol said, warmly.

Jennifer hastily put the phone down and fell onto the sofa, grabbed a cushion and howled into it. Some lovely chap …if only she knew! Her mind drifted back again, remembering the tears of that Thursday morning.

"Why tears?" asked Simon, kissing them away. "Tears of regret?"

"No, oh, no. No regrets. They are of awareness, absolute joy. I have never been loved like that in my whole life."

"And I," said Simon, "have never loved anybody like that." He rested Jennifer's head on his chest of soft curly hairs. "Here we are, totally naked in this bed, having just met and fallen in love."

Her hand touched his chest. Love, yes, love, she thought … having just met and fallen in love. Simon kissed her hair and Jennifer raised her head and kissed him.

"And fallen in love," she said.

He kissed her and they made love again.

Afterwards, they were lying in each other's arms.

"What are we going to do now?" asked Jennifer.

"Well," said Simon, "you've promised your husband his fishing rod, so I suggest we make our way to buying that via some breakfast."

Jennifer got off the bed and, as she did so, he patted her bottom. Jennifer went into the bathroom singing 'April in Paris'.

"You're out of tune!" Simon called to her.

"No, I am not. Come in here and I'll show you!"

He did and they bathed together, Simon throwing bubbles at Jennifer and caressing her breasts with the suds.

"This is fun!" laughed Jennifer. "I've never had a bath with Peter, as he always closes the door and has a private time in the bathroom. He's wonderful and I do love him dearly."

"I know you do. You are a very loving lady."

They eventually got out of the bath and dried each other. Jennifer got dressed in the bedroom, whilst Simon shaved and got dressed in the bathroom. She blow dried her hair and put on a little makeup, then they gathered the things that they required for the day, locked the door and sauntered towards the lift.

"Let's use the stairs," said Jennifer. "I feel like floating down instead of taking the lift."

"Sounds good to me," replied Simon.

Simon handed in the key at reception. "Mr

Green, will you be requiring a table in the Palm Court restaurant this evening?"

For a second, Simon forgot their pseudonym. "Ah, yes!" He turned to Jennifer. "Darling, do we want to eat in the hotel this evening?"

"No, I just want to dance and dance!"

The receptionist smiled at the couple. "Well, this evening, we do have a small quartet playing in the dining room from eight-thirty onwards."

"My wife and I will think about what we'd like to do. Do we have to book?"

"No, sir,"

"Thank you," said Simon.

CHAPTER 9

They were both outside, standing by the green trees and laughing.

"I forgot for a moment!" exclaimed Simon.

"I know! I thought I was going to burst out laughing when you turned around and looked at me."

"Darling, let's just walk and see what our day has in store for us." Jennifer linked her arm into Simon's, thinking how glad she was that they had made love. She felt so close to him as she looked up at him and he put his hand on her arm.

"You're thinking the same thoughts as me, aren't you? How do you know what I'm thinking?" asked Jennifer.

"Yes, I was thinking about when we made love. It was wonderful. Can we do it again?"

"Yes, right now, if you want to - and for the rest of our lives," replied Jennifer. "Oh, wouldn't it be wonderful if it was you and me forever and ever?" They had walked quite a way, oblivious to their surroundings and the hustle and bustle and were now quite a way from the hotel. "But it's ridiculous! You go back to Sussex tomorrow and I go back to Hereford and we both have spouses that we love."

"Yes, I know," said Simon. "But, for now, let's

just enjoy our time together."

They were approaching a little pavement café. "Look!" said Jennifer. "It even has tables and chairs outside - really French." Jennifer sat down. "I think it would be romantic to sit here."

Simon sat down and they huddled together. "Are you cold?"

"Not as long as you cuddle up to me!"

A waiter approached them. "Would you like to order?"

"Yes, please. I'd like to order scrambled egg on wholemeal toast with grilled tomatoes, a large orange juice and a coffee, please," said Jennifer, facing Simon.

"That sounds good. I'll have the same as my wife." The waiter left them.

"Have I told you how lovely you look, darling Jennifer Darling? Very chic in your cosy cashmere scarf and coat. Unfortunately, your trousers are covering up those legs!"

"These were the clothes I wore when I arrived at the airport to fly to Kuwait."

"How did you manage all those suitcases?"

"Peter drove me to the airport because he thought that I would never manage. He was quite right."

Whilst they were waiting for their breakfast to arrive, Simon was musing on when he and Jennifer had first spotted each other. "So, do you think you spied me first at Kuwait Airport?" asked Simon.

"No! I thought you spied me first!" retorted Jennifer.

"I did!" teased Simon. "A mutual attraction," he smiled.

The waiter brought their breakfast and laid it out on their table. "I'm starving," said Jennifer, as she tucked in.

"You most certainly are!" confirmed Simon. They both ate eagerly, hardly saying a word to each other.

The waiter came and cleared away their plates.

"Would you like some more coffee, darling?" asked Simon.

"Oh, yes, please!"

"A large pot and our bill, please," said Simon, as he turned back to Jennifer.

"We don't know much about each other really, even though I feel as though I've always been waiting for you." He cuddled up closer to Jennifer. "When's your birthday? What are your favourite things?"

"Well," said Jennifer, "my birthday is on the twenty-ninth of July."

"You're kidding!"

"No! That was the day I was born!"

"I don't believe it! You're not going to believe it,

but that's my birthday as well!"

"We're twins!" They both laughed out loud.

"Oh, I'm so happy," said Jennifer. "I love being with you."

"And I with you," said Simon as he kissed her with gentle pressure and meaning.

The waiter returned with the bill and the pot of coffee and Simon handed him his card for payment. Whilst pouring the coffee, Simon looked up towards Jennifer.

"Now, where were we? You were saying that your birthday is the same as my birthday, the twenty-ninth of July."

"Yes, the same date as Lady Diana's wedding. Lovely Lady Diana," said Jennifer.

"Yes, that was nineteen eighty-one and my fiftieth birthday." The waiter returned and Simon put his card back in his wallet.

"You don't need a maths degree to work out that I'm having a biggy this year," said Jennifer. "Did you have a big party, as it was your fiftieth?" asked Jennifer.

"Yes, we had a big marquee on the lawn and all the family - cousins I had never seen and didn't know … The boys came, my brother and his wife, Mary. Of course, my dear old mum and pops came, too. It was dad's last year. Mum sadly died the following year from a broken heart. They were inseparable and loved each other very much.

"Oh, I'm so sorry."

"It was a very sad eighteen months. Lovely old people. Why do they have to leave us?" Jennifer was sipping her coffee, listening attentively and looking into his lovely, caring eyes. "What did you do the day of the royal wedding?" he asked.

"I watched the whole ceremony from start to finish! I had some girlfriends around. We drank champagne and toasted the lovely couple. I thought that Diana looked like a fairy princess in her beautiful gown and her shining tiara." Jennifer smiled. "It looked like stars around her head… And, then, in the evening, as it was my birthday, we all went out to my favourite restaurant."

The pair of them were enjoying the coffee and each other's company, whilst musing over their shared birthday. "Did you have a disco in the evening, or perhaps an orchestra?" asked Jennifer.

"An orchestra?"

"Just joking!" laughed Jennifer.

"I like teasing you, too," said Simon. "Actually, we did have a disco."

Jennifer was sipping her mug of coffee, looking at him over the rim of the cup and shaking her head softly. "Does your wife like to dance?"

"Yes, she's quite good."

"Not as good as me, I bet," teased Jennifer.

"Do I detect a little jealousy?"

She nudged his leg. "Maybe!"

They got up from the table and walked away, arm in arm. "Isn't it a lovely day? The sun is even shining for us. You know what they say: the sun always shines on the righteous… I think we ought to get the fishing rod now," said Jennifer, "before I completely forget."

They walked along, enjoying the April sunshine.

"Harrods is not too far," said Simon as he pointed out various places of interest to Jennifer. She thought him so sweet, just like one of those tour guides.

They walked through Belgravia to Sloane Square and into Knightsbridge. Simon looked at his watch and put his hand onto Jennifer's.

"My darling, we met exactly twelve hours ago. Just before I boarded the plane, I glanced at my watch. It was ten-fourteen; ten-fifteen, when I was standing by your seat. How could we have imagined this? You and I are buying your husband's birthday present here in Harrods." He took Jennifer's arm and they swept through the doors. "Now, which department?"

"Fishing rod department!" replied Jennifer, giving him a gentle elbow in the ribs. "There's a store guide," she pointed. "Leisure Pursuits - there, that floor!" They made their way to the lifts.

Jennifer was glancing around. "You know, I always love coming to Harrods whenever I come to London. They say that, if you stand at the entrance of this store for a week ... or is it a year? ...that you'll see somebody you know."

"Let's hope that doesn't happen today!" declared Simon, as they entered the lift.

"No, that would be awful!" agreed Jennifer.

"Are you ashamed of me?" Simon asked with a smile. "Here we are! Fishing rod section." They walked into the department. "So many fishing rods! Who would have thought it? Let's find the perfect one and get out of here."

They approached the counter, where a very nice gentleman greeted them with a smile. "Good morning." The politeness in his voice reminded Jennifer of Simon's receptionist on the phone.

I really must pull myself together! I'll make myself another mug of coffee and then go and see Bess and take her for a ride. It was a showery April day, but perfect for a ride. She remembered telling Simon about her beloved animals when they were buying the fishing rod...

"I'm looking for a fishing rod for my, uh, brother."

"Whoops, that was close!" whispered Simon into

her ear.

"I know! I almost let the side down, didn't I?" admitted Jennifer.

"These are some of our most popular ones over here," said the assistant. They walked over to the stand where the rods were. "I will leave you to have a look, Madam."

"Do you fish?" asked Simon, as he picked up a rod and replaced it.

"Yes, I have been known to, but I prefer to ride my lovely horse, Bess. We go out every day. Of course, we are accompanied by Chi Chi, my dog." They were looking at the fishing rods. "Eeny, meeny, miny…we'll take this one." Decision made, she and Simon returned to the counter.

"A good choice, if I might say, Madam. I'm sure your brother will enjoy his present."

"Is there any chance you could arrange for it to be delivered to The Ritz sometime this afternoon?" enquired Simon. "My wife and I are visitors and don't want to be bogged down carrying it around."

"Certainly, your name?"

"Mr and Mrs Green, room twenty-four."

"That will be done," said the assistant, while finishing off the transaction and handing Jennifer the receipt. "Enjoy the rest of your stay."

"Thank you, we most certainly will. Goodbye," he replied. Simon and Jennifer walked out of the department.

"What a clever idea! You are a well-seasoned shopper!" said Jennifer.

"I do frequently have packages delivered to my office. Now I would like to buy you something as a memento."

"I don't want anything. The memory of you and me together will live in my heart forever."

"Just a little one, please?" implored Simon.

"Oh, all right, but not jewellery. That would be a little difficult to explain… I know! A plane!"

"A plane?" questioned Simon, pulling out a chair. They had wandered around the floors chatting and found themselves at the refreshment bar. "You might think that I have pots of money, but a plane is stretching it a little!"

"Not a real one, silly," she laughed and removed her coat.

"I know. I was only teasing!"

"A toy Jumbo," explained Jennifer, sitting down.

Simon put his jacket on top of her coat. "A Jumbo jet? Yes, of course! We met on a Jumbo," he said, finally following Jennifer's train of thought.

"That's the memento I would like."

"Okay, and I'll buy one for myself, so, every time we look at them, we can be reminded of our wonderful meeting," said Simon.

Jennifer was in her sitting room. She got up and walked towards the mantle shelf and there it was: her little silver Jumbo jet. She picked it up.

"That's a nice gift to bring back from Kuwait," said Peter when he saw it.

"I thought it would commemorate the birth of Noah and, when they come home, he will see it on the mantelpiece." She put it down gently. What a lie! And I have to lie again. I will attend the funeral, so I can say goodbye properly and see his lovely family. I could ask Carol to come with me and stay in a little hotel just outside the village. I must speak to her, she thought, as her hand lingered on the plane.

CHAPTER 10

Their tall glasses of fruit juice duly arrived. "Thank you. I'm quite thirsty."

"Me, too," said Simon.

They drank their juice.

"Now for those planes. Porcelain department maybe?" suggested Jennifer.

"No, silver," said Simon. "The colour of the plane."

They found the appropriate department. "There, look!" There were all kinds of planes displayed in a cabinet in the middle of the room. "But I can only see one Jumbo," said Jennifer, disappointed.

"I'm sure they'll have more in the stockroom," Simon reassured her. He was right.

"Would you like them gift-wrapped, sir?" the lady behind the counter asked.

"Yes, please. I want to give one of them to a very special friend."

The assistant took payment and handed Simon a Harrods bag with two beautifully wrapped identical parcels inside. As they walked out of the department, Simon put the small bag into his right-hand jacket pocket so he could put his arm around Jennifer. "I feel really good about what we've just bought," he said, as he kissed her head.

They were standing outside on the pavement. "What would you like to do now?"

"I'd like to have a snooze sometime this afternoon, so that I can be nice and refreshed for this evening," Jennifer replied.

"Good idea! Let's walk through the park on our way back to the hotel."

They entered Kensington Gardens and watched the people walking their dogs and babies being pushed in prams. They sat down on a bench. A lady on a chestnut mare rode past and nodded her head. "Lovely day." They both said 'yes' in unison. His grip around her shoulders tightened. Her coat felt warm in the sunshine. Jennifer watched as the lady rode farther away.

"Thoughts?" asked Simon.

"I was just thinking about my Bess. I haven't seen her for three weeks - or my Chi Chi. I hope they're missing me. Bess is black and shiny, a beautiful lady. She can hear me coming in the morning and stamps her feet as I approach her stable. Then she neighs as I call good morning and eagerly stands by the door. Chi Chi is always by my side. She's a lovely spaniel - black and white with floppy ears and huge lovely eyes. I love them both so very much."

They got up from the bench. Simon put his arm around Jennifer and pulled her closer as they continued their walk through the park.

"Do you have a dog?" she asked.

"Yes, I have two. They're also spaniels. Chocolate and cream."

"What are their names?"

"Bruce and Bill. They're brothers and twelve years old - quite an age." The Serpentine came into view. "How about hiring a rowing boat?" suggested Simon.

"I would like that very much!"

As they were strolling, they were enjoying finding out more about each other. "Tell me more about your dogs. I want to know everything," said Jennifer.

"My life's history?" Simon linked her arm in his and rested his hand on hers. "The boys, as I call them, often both sit on the step leading into the porch of our house and can hear the car as I sweep into the drive. They always wait until the car has stopped and then rush for their greeting. Sylvie has a cat, a huge monster of a thing, long ginger hair, and I am sure he snarls at me. He only has eyes for her. When we're watching television, he's always there, curled up on her lap and she strokes him and, just occasionally, I wish that she did that to me. She dotes on that cat."

Jennifer laughed. "Poor Simon!"

"Do you know what they call this drive?" asked

Simon.

"Carriage Drive."

"How did you know that?"

"I've just seen the sign!" She kissed his cheek. "Sounds very romantic, but we don't have a carriage, only a rowing boat! So, come and show me your rowing skills!" He helped Jennifer into the boat and gave it a shove away from the side of the lake. Simon removed his jacket, took hold of the oars and started to row.

"I just hope I can row and talk at the same time, sitting opposite such a lovely lady!"

As Simon began rowing, Jennifer was watching his strong arms move with the strokes of the oars. "Do you make love very often?" asked Jennifer.

"Well, only in the mating season! Where did that come from?"

"I was just thinking about you and her and what we are becoming with each other." "Profound words indeed! You have been brewing that up, haven't you?" said Simon.

"Yes - well, no."

"Do you with Peter?"

"I asked you first!" replied Jennifer, laughing. "Well, Peter has never been romantic. I knew this when I met him, but he has always been very kind to me and an exceptional father to Lydia." She was trailing her hand through the water. "I have always been reasonably happy... Please don't think that I'm criticising him. I must sound so unhappy, but, after this morning, you've shown me what my life could have been." She took her hand out of the water and flicked some droplets at Simon. "You beast! Until yesterday, I was quite content and now I have something truly wonderful to miss!" She started to cry. Simon placed the oars by his side and gingerly made his way towards her. He sat down next to her, picked up an oar, placed it in the water and started to move it, gently guiding the boat.

"More tears," he said.

"I'm sorry. I'm really trying to be brave, knowing that this is only pretend, but the fact of the matter is, my darling Simon, I'm falling in love with you." His lips found hers and they kissed with a deep knowing, his arm firmly around her shoulder and squeezing her closely to him.

CHAPTER 11

Jennifer was awakened from the memory of boating with Simon by the sound of a car pulling up outside. "Oh, Chi, who's that? We're in no mood for visitors!" She peeped through the kitchen window. Dash! It's Carol. Oh, I must look dreadful, she thought.

Carol knocked on the door. Unusual for her, thought Jennifer as she opened the door.

"You sounded dreadful! I just had to come over and see you and simply find out what is wrong. You look like death! Has something happened?" asked Carol anxiously, as she entered the kitchen.

"I'm glad you're here," replied Jennifer. "Would you walk over to the stable with me to let Bess out?"

"Goodness!" exclaimed Carol. "It must be something serious for you not to let Bess out until now." Jennifer was trying hard to control her emotions. "Well, tell me!" urged Carol, as she turned Jennifer around to face her. "You've met someone in Kuwait, haven't you? And you're in love - so much so that you don't know how to tell Peter!"

"Let's go and see Bess," said Jennifer, "and I'll tell you all about it when we come back." Jennifer grabbed a coat from the hook on the back door.

"Okay. How's the baby?" Carol asked as she put the kettle on, ready for their return.

"Oh, he's gorgeous! Looks just like Liddy."

"So, he takes after his grandma! Did you do lots of parties?" asked Carol.

"A few." They closed the door behind them and walked through the yard towards the stable. Bess could hear Jennifer approaching and started to stamp her foot and neigh - rather louder than normal, perhaps. She can sense my sadness, Jennifer thought.

"Does she always make that racket?" asked Carol.

"Yes. She's just saying hello… Hello, my lovely!" She opened the door and Bess came over to her and nestled into her chest. Jennifer looked into her beautiful eyes. "Forgive me," she said quietly and tapped her on her velvety nose.

"Breakfast, Bess?" Carol was standing there with some oats.

"I think she just wants to go outside. She can have that later," said Jennifer. Bess followed them through the door and hurried into the field. "I'll leave her door open." She gave her fresh water. "Thank you for that, Carol. I just didn't know how I was going to have the strength to let her out. I was even contemplating phoning Tom's wife."

"Tom. Faithful old Tom and Margaret. They've been with you for years. They were very lucky that your father-in-law left them his cottage."

"Yes, I know, but they're wonderful and jolly well deserve it in payment for their loyalty over the years," Jennifer replied.

"Come on. I can see that you have a lot to tell me." Carol linked her arm into Jennifer's as they walked back to the farmhouse. The kettle had boiled and Carol took two huge mugs from the cupboard. "Steaming coffee. That's what we need!"

Jennifer took two chairs from the kitchen table and placed them in front of the Rayburn, opening its door so that she could gain a little comfort from the warmth of the fire. She started to cry.

"You did meet someone in Kuwait, didn't you? Is he a Kuwaiti?"

"No, he was English."

"Was! What do you mean?"

"He was killed on his way back home on Friday."

Carol gasped. "Oh, Jennifer!"

"We met on the plane. Well, actually, we met at the airport. Liddy sort of introduced us. Oh, Carol, I must go to his funeral. I just want to be near him one more time. I have to go. I just don't know how to tell Peter! He wouldn't bat an eyelid, I know, but I'd feel as though I'd be... oh, it's just too difficult!"

"If it really means that much to you, I'll come with you!"

"You would do that for me?"

"Yes, of course. What are friends for? I'll book us both into a hotel near where the funeral is and you can say your goodbyes. Now have your coffee." Carol took the two mugs from the table and handed one to Jennifer. "Tell me all about it."

"We sat next to each other on the plane. He was so attentive. I fell in love immediately and he with me. We left the sleepers and went up into the bar. He bought champagne. We enjoyed each other's company so much that, before the plane landed, we had already made up our minds that we were going to spend the whole of Thursday and part of Friday together."

"Including the night?" asked Carol.

"Yes. We made love as soon as the porter closed the door! He took me to heights I've only read about in books - a fantastic lover."

"Weren't you both embarrassed showing all your bits?"

"No, no, it was wonderful! He made me aware of bits that I didn't know I had! Oh, Carol, I loved him. I genuinely loved him. I love Peter, too, as you know, and, once this is over on Friday, I'll get back to normality with the christening and everything."

"I know you will." Carol finished her coffee.

"Things to do, people to meet!"

Jennifer laughed. "You always say that!"

"I knew I would get a smile out of you."

"Thank you so much for coming, Carol."

"No problem. I don't suppose we'll see you tonight."

"No, I don't think so. Might be different if it was just you and me."

"Let the boys go! They can have their food and play darts and I'll come here about eight. We can have a drink of wine and I'll bring some supper for us both, so you don't have to cook."

"I'd really like that. We'll settle down in the sitting room in front of the fire and have a good chat," said Jennifer as she kissed Carol on the cheek. "See you later."

She closed the door and hung her coat back up on its hook, picked up the mugs and put them in the dishwasher. Chi Chi was at her feet, looking up at her with eager eyes. Jennifer stooped down and stroked her lovingly. "Ah, you're my dear friend as well." She made herself another mug of coffee and sat down. Chi Chi got onto her lap and enjoyed the warmth. Jennifer sipped her coffee and looked into the fire. "I'm glad that Carol knows. She's a good friend, isn't she, Chi?" Chi Chi was asleep, all snuggled and warm - just like I was with Simon's arms around me, thought Jennifer, sadly.

CHAPTER 12

"I love you, Jennifer. I can't explain what's happened to us. These things do happen to people. Two perfect strangers meet and, a couple of hours later, they're beginning to think that they are not going to be able to live without each other. The journey we'd have in front of us, if you were willing to take it with me, my darling Jennifer! It would anger and upset a lot of friends and family. They would think us completely mad, but we only have one life, my darling."

"I know," said Jennifer. "It's far too new and painful to think about right now. I would prefer to talk about it later. It worries me what could happen and, as you say, the hurt that we both could cause."

A duck quacked loudly as it swam past their boat with five little ducklings. Jennifer and Simon laughed. "Look, she's blowing her horn," said Jennifer. "She's telling you to get out of her way!"

"Bad rower - especially with one oar!" exclaimed Simon and gingerly made his way back down the boat. As he did, Jennifer slapped his bottom.

"I couldn't resist!"

Simon sat back down. "Just you wait till later!" He picked up the oars and started to row.

"Can we go in now?" asked Jennifer.

"Yes, we'll go and have some lunch."

"…and sleep," added Jennifer.

"Well, that was not quite what I had in mind!"

"No, I mean afterwards!" Jennifer looked at him with her head to one side.

"Over here, guv! You can bring her in here." Simon navigated towards where the man was indicating, threw him the rope and they were pulled towards the mooring. Simon leaned forward and, taking Jennifer's hand, gently helped her out of the boat.

"Thank you, goodbye! That was fun!" said Jennifer.

"Would you like some lunch now?" asked Simon.

"No, I'm not hungry. I'd like to go back to our room. We've both been up for a long time. You're so sweet, entertaining me - you must be exhausted," said Jennifer.

"Yes, I am, but I don't want to miss a moment - we have so little time together."

They walked arm in arm. "There's Kensington Palace," said Jennifer, pointing, "Isn't it a lovely house? What's your house like? Does your wife like the same things that you like?"

"Well," he squeezed her hand, "we have had our home a long time. My father was the local solicitor and used to run his practice from his home and, when Sylvie and I started to pour out of our house, my parents suggested we moved by swapping houses. We were in practice together and we all agreed that it would be a good idea. I must say it worked out fine and, when my father died, we and my other partners approached my uncle, who had a small Victorian house in Pimlico. He wanted to retire and live in France, so we bought the house from him and now run the practice from there."

"All very interesting," said Jennifer, "but that doesn't tell me anything about your house. I want to visualise you there: your favourite chair and where you might place your Jumbo."

"I'll tell you exactly where I'll place him. I have a tallboy in my dressing room and that will be its home. I'll be able to see it while I'm getting dressed and when I'm having my bath."

"You have a bath in you dressing room?"

"Yes, it's just through an arch and I can see my tallboy."

"Well, I'll put mine on the mantelpiece in the sitting room. It's my favourite room in the house. I love it. In the winter, we have a roaring fire and then, in the summer, we open the French doors and sit on the terrace, where we barbecue. Peter thinks he's a culinary master as far as cooking outside goes. I prepare the food and he cooks. Nothing to it,

65

he says. He does amuse me."

"I bet you're a good cook," said Simon.

"I love cooking and enjoy having dinner parties."

"I'd like to come to one of those," said Simon, squeezing her arm.

"I wish you could," said Jennifer.

"Sylvie doesn't like cooking. I do the cooking in our house. I enjoy messing about and trying to follow the recipe book word for word. I'm always very pleased when our friends say how much they've enjoyed it."

"Doesn't your wife mind you getting all the praise?"

"No. She's one of those modern women."

"I'd want to do everything for you, so that you'd be proud of me and all my accomplishments," said Jennifer.

"I'll be very proud of you, if the situation ever happens. It's up to you. Sylvie and I live very different lives." They were outside the hotel already. "I'll get the key. Would you like me to order some lunch?"

"Yes, please,"

"What would you like?"

"Smoked salmon sandwiches on wholemeal bread with fresh orange juice, please."

Simon ordered lunch with a chilled bottle of

Chablis 'to our room'. "Certainly, Mr Green."

They got into the lift and Jennifer put her head on Simon's chest. "I could sleep. Suddenly, I'm very tired."

"Nearly there. Then we can both sleep for a couple of hours." Simon opened the door and Jennifer removed her coat, threw herself on the bed and removed her shoes.

"Oh, that's better!"

Simon removed his jacket, joined Jennifer on the bed and removed his shoes. Jennifer moved closer. Simon put his arm around her. As she lay her head on his chest, they both fell asleep with Jennifer nuzzling his lovely warm sweater. They did not hear the porter bring up the lunch.

CHAPTER 13

"Wake up, chicken! Wakey, wakey!"

"Oh, I'm sorry, darling. I must have fallen asleep."

"And you've broken your mug! Are you all right?" Jennifer was quite hazy, having just awakened from her memories. "It hasn't affected you this way before." Peter, disturbed by her stress, came towards her and held her.

"Perhaps you need a tonic. Go along and see the old doc."

"Yes, yes, I'll do that. You're so thoughtful, Peter."

"Must look after my little chickadee! What would I do without you? Have you had any lunch?"

"No, I just nodded off. I don't even know the time. Two-thirty! Gosh! I've been asleep for about two hours!"

"I'll make you a sandwich."

"No, thanks. Peter. I'm really not hungry."

"A cup of coffee?"

"No, thank you, darling, but I would like an orange juice." She watched him as he went over to the fridge and opened the door.

"Here, poppet, drink this."

"I'm feeling much better now. I needed that

sleep."

"My mother used to say the world is a different place after a good sleep!"

"You are funny, Peter!" She put her glass on the table and kissed him.

"What was that for - in the middle of the day?"

"Exactly," she said. "I'm going to have a bath now and freshen myself up. Do you mind if I don't come this evening? I don't think I'd be very good company and, besides that, Carol is coming over and bringing supper."

"No, you do what you want. You can always show the photographs next week. You'll enjoy Carol's company and have a really good chin wag, I'm sure." Jennifer was in the hall, making her way to the staircase. "Don't bother about food for me," Peter called from the kitchen. "I'll eat at the pub."

"No, I'll rustle you up ham, egg and chips."

"No, you have a night off. It's just nice having you home. Go and have your bath. We've got a few lambs beginning to arrive, so I'll be back about five. Okay? Bye!"

Jennifer climbed the stairs and was feeling much better after her sleep. She entered their bedroom, went into the bathroom, ran her bath, putting her favourite smellies under the running water and looked out of the window. There was Bess, eating the new summer grass. She looked splendid in the afternoon sunshine. She slipped into the bath and enjoyed the warmth. When you're feeling sad, you enjoy warmth. I remember when Daddy died, I spent all day in the bath and all night by the fire and even took a hot water bottle to bed. Nearly two years. Oh, how I miss him! She finished her bath and wrapped herself in a large fluffy towel, went into her bedroom and lay on the bed.

"I've been watching you sleep for ages," Simon said.

"I hope I didn't snore like a baby pig!"

"Yes, but I didn't care. It's not important anyway," he said, moving towards her lips. "You were sleeping soundly."

He kissed her and she knew by his kiss that they were going to make love. He removed Jennifer's sweater and she started to remove his top. Simon unbuttoned her blouse button by button, gently kissing her lips as he removed her blouse and then her bra. Jennifer lay back so that he could remove her trousers and panties. She was naked on their bed. He quickly removed the rest of his clothes, amusing Jennifer as he did so. Then he threw himself on top of her and slipped inside her. He was very hard and she could tell that he just could not wait - and neither could she. He moved with such force, as if he could not get enough of her. She lifted her legs and wrapped them around him as he sighed in her ear. He kissed her lips.

"Oh, Jenny, I love you! Let's make love forever." He kissed her again and then he climaxed. Oh, how he ejaculated!

Oh, Simon, I love you so much, she thought. Afterwards, their bodies were moist.

"I'm sorry," said Simon. "I just couldn't wait. I wanted to do that on the lake."

"So did I."

They were glistening with sweat. She rubbed her hand over the wet hairs on his chest. "Am I really here?" asked Jennifer. "Have I actually committed adultery?"

Simon turned to Jennifer. "We both have. Are you regretting it?"

"No," answered Jennifer. "I do feel a little guilty, though - do you?"

"Yes, but only a little bit - hardly noticeable at all."

"You're a wicked man, Simon!"

"I know! Isn't it fun, just being ourselves and enjoying everything about each other?" He picked up the phone. "I'll ring down to reception and ask if we can have our lunch sent up."

"Oh, and a pot of tea, please," added Jennifer.

She went into the bathroom. Simon followed her. "I told reception that my wife and I had fallen asleep."

"I wonder if they believe that we're married," mused Jennifer.

"Indeed they do! I bet they've never had a more normal married couple staying in this hotel." He kissed her neck. Her anxious nipple received his lips with delight as he pulled it into his mouth and sucked it gently like a baby. His hand went down between her legs and caressed her clitoris. She could feel herself slipping away. His fingers entered her and penetrated her vagina. He moved over to her other nipple, removed his fingers and touched her clitoris, rubbing it gently. Jennifer could not hold herself back any longer. She climaxed with enormous pleasure. He gently laid her on her towel on the floor and then positioned himself beside her. She knew that it was her turn now to pleasure Simon. She lifted herself up and lay between his lovely, hairy legs. She kissed his lips and moved down his body. She kissed his curly chest, sliding over to his nipples. She put his nipple in her mouth and moved her tongue around it. It felt lovely while touching his over-swollen penis and moving her hand up and down his shiny member. Her mouth moved closer to his eager body. She took his penis into her mouth, sucking him gently. She then rose and lowered her body onto him, swallowing him as he went deeper and deeper inside her. His hands came up towards her and pinched her nipples with his fingers. Simon was moving quite rapidly. They both were moving together. Jennifer leaned back and put her hands behind her, resting them on his legs as he climaxed again with such force Jennifer that thought she was going to end up on the ceiling. She lay on his chest, still attached to him. They lay there until he was ready for Jennifer to slide off. She lifted herself from between his legs and lay on the towel by his side. They turned their heads and looked into each other's eyes. Jennifer could see what was in his eyes. He kissed her lips softly.

She got up from the towel, grabbing another towel and closed it around her. Simon was still lying on the floor. She walked into the bedroom. Juices started pouring from her love. She reluctantly dabbed between her legs with a tissue.

"We've missed lunch again," Jennifer called out to Simon, who was still lying on the floor. She removed her silk dressing gown from her suitcase and put the towel on the chair.

"No," he said. "I told them I'd call when we were ready." Simon came into the bedroom totally starkers. Jennifer grabbed her towel and wrapped it around him.

"Keeps temptation at bay for a little while," she said.

Simon picked up the phone. "Hello. This is Mr

Green. Will you please send our order up now?" Turning to Jennifer, he said, "When I'm back in my office on Monday morning and somebody says 'Mr Lawson', I'll wonder who the hell they're talking to! You little minx! You did this to me! You've made me totally confused about my life. Come here." He put his arms around her waist. "Seriously, what are we going to do?"

"We've found each other. Please don't say any more," said Jennifer. "My heart aches when you say things like that. Let's just enjoy our time here together." She smiled. "Tomorrow's another day."

There was a knock at the door. "Saved by the bell – well, a knock anyway," said Simon, as he went to open the door. The waiter rolled into the room with a lovely, dressed trolley. "Will you please put it by the sofa?" Simon thanked the waiter and gave him a tip.

"Thank you, Mr Green. Enjoy your lunch," said the waiter as he left the room and closed the door. We certainly will, thought Jennifer, moving towards the food.

Simon removed the towel and replaced it with his dressing gown from his suitcase. He tied it as he walked towards Jennifer and picked up a pretty cup and saucer. "How do you take your tea, Madam: lemon or cream?"

"Lemon, please."

He poured her tea and handed it to her, which she drank immediately. "I was thirsty," said Jennifer, as she picked up a sandwich. "When we were making love in the bathroom, you called me Jenny."

"Yes, I did. Why? Don't you like being called Jenny?"

She put down her plate. "My darling Simon, I loved you calling me Jenny. It sounded so perfect coming from you. Daddy called me Jenny, too. It was his pet name for me, as well as 'Butterfly'."

"Is your mother still alive?"

"No, she died last June. It was a very sad time and I still find it difficult to talk about her. I still can't believe that she's no longer here - neither Mummy or Daddy." Simon gave her hand an extra squeeze. "Peter wanted to name our daughter after me, so we chose my second name, Lydia. Two Jennifers would have been too much." She smiled.

"I love talking and finding out about you," Simon said, as he poured her another cup of tea and kissed her cheek.

"Tell me more about your life in Sussex. I want to know so many things about you. What's your house like? What's your taste in furniture?" Jennifer was keen to know more about this wonderful man's life.

"Well..." Simon was holding Jennifer gently.

"When we swapped houses, my mother took with her the smaller family items and we inherited the rest, as our furniture wasn't suitable for The Oaks."

"Sounds very grand," said Jennifer.

"Yes, it is. It stands very boldly in the centre of the village, surrounded by a high wall. The grounds are full of old oak trees. Sylvie insisted that a few were chopped down a few years ago to bring more light into the house. Oh, and we created a croquet lawn."

"I can see how content you are," said Jennifer reluctantly.

"Content, yes," answered Simon.

They had finished their sandwiches. He opened the wine and handed Jennifer a glass. They clinked. No words were necessary. They both knew what the other was thinking.

"So, tell me about Hereford. I've never been there. We southerners seem to stay put."

"It's a pretty market town and has a wonderful cathedral. The river Wye runs through it. In fact, it runs near our farm. That's where Peter does his fishing. He owns a run of water. Both banks were given to him by his father for his twenty-first birthday. The farm is a family-run business - a bit like yours, only we're into farming and you're into what you're into."

"Law. Corporate law mostly. My brother dabbles

in wills and the like and the other partner is a lawyer for court cases."

"The farmhouse is a typical red farmhouse for that area: square, quite large and we have a drive that sweeps up to the house. We do also have a back drive that goes through the farmyard. The front door is one of my favourite aspects of the house. It is huge and half- glazed, so that, when the lights are on and you're coming home in the evening, it welcomes you."

"You old romantic, you," Simon teased.

"I am, aren't I?" she said, nudging him with her finger. "There's a large hall with a wide staircase in front of you. I love to float down those stairs when I have one of my lovely ball gowns on. We go to rather a lot of functions, as Peter is chairman of this and that. He's also president of our local rugby club and past captain of the golf club." She stopped. "What are you staring at?"

"I'm just imagining you in one of those ball gowns. I bet you look stunning. I would love to see you in one."

"I do have a cocktail dress with me." She put down her glass and went over to her suitcases. "Here it is." She hung it up in the wardrobe. "I think that will be perfect for this evening. It has a pretty jacket as well."

"And pretty shoes?" asked Simon. She walked

over to him and sat down. He put his arm around her and pulled her closer to him. "Tell me more."

"I love flowers," she said. "I always have arrangements in the hall, sitting room and dining room - also sometimes in our bedroom, too, though they make Peter sneeze. He asks me what I want 'those wretched things' for." She laughed. "He removes them, but I put them back when he stops sneezing. Then he realises they are back and says he'll never understand why I like them and gives me an enormous hug. His tummy rests on his belt these days, so all I can feel is his overhang."

Simon smiled and stood up, looking at his watch.

CHAPTER 14

"Cherub, wakey wakey! Cherub, you nodded off again, didn't you?"

"Oh, I'm so sorry, Peter."

"It's six o'clock, my cherub, and you're still in your towel from your bath earlier." He had brought her a pot of tea. She sat up and took the cup and saucer from him.

"Thank you, darling."

"Mrs Tompkins didn't come today. I found a note by the back door. Apparently, her mother's sister has died."

"Gosh!" said Jennifer. "Poor lady! Though I'd completely forgotten that she was due to come." Peter sat on the bed next to her. "Didn't you bring yourself a cup?" she asked.

"No, I had one with the boys before I came home."

"How many lambs are there?"

"Six overnight. The others will now be gathered and put in the birthing barn, so that we can take turns in looking after the ewes and their lambs. When I came through the farmyard, I noticed that Bess was in her stable, so I gave her some fresh bedding and closed the door."

"Oh, thank you."

Jennifer went into the bathroom just down the landing. Six o'clock. That was the time that Simon had said: to think this time tomorrow, Bill and Bruce will be waiting for me at home. Jennifer had then scolded him.

"I don't want to talk about us parting," she had said quite sharply. "Please don't." Simon was facing her.

"We won't." He had kissed her tenderly. "Jenny, Jenny, my one true love." Jennifer had then started to cry.

"Another bath?" asked Peter, as he came through the bathroom door.

"Yes, I feel so chilly," she said, trying to avoid looking at him, just in case he could see that she was crying.

"Are you feeling feverish?" He felt her forehead. "You're crying!"

"It must be the change," she said.

"You'll have to get yourself off to the doc for some of that H something or other."

"Yes, I'll do that."

"You're a silly goose, aren't you?"

"Yes," she said and smiled.

"I'm going to help the boys and I'll be back about seven. Cheer up! As my grandma used to say: chin up!"

Simon lifted her head towards his lips. He kissed all her tears away. "Is that better?"

"Yes," said Jennifer.

They went into the bathroom together and, whilst Simon was leaning over the bath, she could see the strength in his legs and thighs and lovely bottom.

"Would madam like this in her bath?" he asked, holding up a bottle of bubbles. She nodded.

"I'd like you to have my address and office telephone number," he said as he got into the bath at the opposite end to Jennifer.

"I thought that this was only going to be a one-night stand."

"Well, I wouldn't have put it quite like that, although I have done a lot of 'standing' since we met." He looked at the water and, sure enough, his 'stance' was peeping out. She could see that he was always pleased to see her! Leaning towards Jennifer, Simon said, "I never want this to end. I want us to have a future together. To be in love, make love for always, have a home…"

"Stop, please stop!" she interrupted him. "I could never leave Peter. I'm his whole life and he depends on me for everything."

"Exactly," said Simon. "He depends on you and what do you get in return? Security, a nice home and lovely friends. You can have all that with me,

Jenny - and more."

"You're serious, aren't you, Simon?"

"I've never been more sincere about a situation like this in my life. I want you for me. I love you." He leaned forward, his eyes quite glossy. "Will you think about it, please? I know that you have to consider Peter."

"I do. He's my best friend." She got out of the bath and grabbed a towel from the rail, quite pleased that it was warm, and walked into the bedroom, closing the door behind her. Simon was silent in the bathroom. She got a few extra things out of one of the cases: her shoes and her shawl. It was April and she was hoping, wherever they were going, that she didn't have to wear her camel coat - it would ruin the effect of her pretty dress. Simon came in from the bathroom, his towel around his hips. Jennifer was leaning over the bed, laying out her clothing. He came towards her very sheepishly.

"I'm so sorry, my darling Jenny. We won't talk about it again. The subject is closed."

"The subject is closed, my darling Simon." She sat down at the dressing table and Simon spotted that she was wearing a suspender belt. He picked up the pair of stockings and more delicate underwear from the bed and passed it all to her.

"What's a poor chap like me going to do? I won't be able to control myself." He sat on the chair and watched as she put on her bra and then her suspender belt. She took the stockings out of their packaging and sat down on the stool, lifting her leg so that her toe could receive her stocking. He peeked under his towel, "Oh, oh, it's happening again!" He dropped the towel onto the floor and, of course, Jennifer could not resist. She urgently sat astride him and he moved slowly. I've never made love on a chair before, thought Jennifer. It was lovely. His legs supported her. As he raised his thighs, she sighed more and more.

"I love your sighs," he said. Holding her close, he could smell the sweet scent of her love misting over her body. He kissed her lips and lingered there while they were gently hugging each other. Jennifer slowly got off his lap and Simon stood up from the chair. He picked up his towel. "Just going into the bathroom, my love. Think of me while I'm away."

…Think of him… I've done nothing else since we parted on Friday, she thought. She had been eager to phone him with her decision.

Jennifer went into the bathroom, where Simon was starting to shave. She sat astride the bidet and started running the water, letting the whole of her fanny soak up the warm spray. "How often do you shave?"

"Once usually, but sometimes twice." She liked watching him shave whilst she was sitting on the bidet. "We're like an old married couple," said Simon, turning around. Her thoughts exactly. We're telepathic, she thought and smiled. She left Simon in the bathroom, removed her dress from the wardrobe, pleased that it was not creased. She hung it on the door, put the shawl around it and stood back. Yes, that will look very pretty. Simon entered.

"You smell nice," said Jennifer.

"It's my aftershave. Expensive. I always buy it in duty-free."

"Smells sexy." She touched his chin. "I'm going into the bathroom to do girly things." She closed the door and saw that there was a hair dryer. She tidied her hair using spray and titivation, took out her mascara and compact, lipstick and eye shadow. Then she sprayed a liberal amount of perfume on and gathered her bits and pieces. She put a few in her make-up case, thinking that perhaps she might need them during the evening. She didn't realise the time and, when she came through the door, there he was in a beautiful dark suit - not the one he was wearing yesterday. It was coupled with a crisp white shirt and a royal blue tie and very shiny shoes.

"Does madam approve?"

"Oh, yes, indeed she does!" Jennifer said,

admiring him as she was putting a few things in her bag. He removed her dress from its hanger and handed it to her. She stepped into it and turned around.

"Would you like it zipped up, madam?"

"Yes, please." She went to her jewellery case, which was on the dressing table, and removed her pearl earrings from her ears, replacing them with her diamond studs. She decided not to wear her necklace, as she did not want to feel overdressed. Finally, she put on her jacket and picked up her wrap and bag.

Simon was standing by the door. "I've been thinking... We'll go and have cocktails before dinner. I know just the place." He guided her to the lift. "You look stunning - and so pretty." At reception, they handed in their key. "What time did you say the Latin music started?" he asked the receptionist.

"From eight-thirty, sir."

"I think that sounds like a good idea, don't you?" he said, turning to Jennifer. "Cocktails, supper and dancing!"

Outside the hotel, the doorman stood out in the road and hailed them a taxi.

"'Copacabana', please, driver," said Simon, as he gently helped Jennifer step in.

It was a chilly night and Jennifer pulled her wrap

around her shoulders. Simon handed her a piece of paper. "There's no need to say anything. I just want you to have this." He closed her fingers gently around the piece of paper. She knew that it was the address and telephone number of his office. She put it in her bag.

CHAPTER 15

The bath was getting cold, so Jennifer got out with no idea of the time. She slipped on her towelling dressing gown and went into the bedroom. My goodness! The time! All I seem to have done all day is just bring back those lovely memories. She looked at the clock: six-forty-five. I must get dressed very quickly, she thought.

She pulled out of her wardrobe a pair of tweed trousers and a crushed strawberry cashmere sweater - the one she had worn with Simon. She smelt it and caught the vague hint of his cologne. She decided to wear it and never to wash it ever again. She grabbed her shoes, put on her socks, went out onto the landing, rushed down the stairs and went into the sitting room. The fire had been lit by Peter. He came in from the kitchen.

"I couldn't hear a sound and thought you might have nodded off again. I know you love a fire and, though it may be the start of summer, it's still pretty chilly in the evenings."

"Thank you! I was rushing downstairs to light one and you've done it for me." Jennifer sat in the nice, cosy armchair by the fire.

"Pumpkin, would you like a drink?" he asked.

"Oh, yes, please! That's just what I need."

"One large gin and tonic coming up!"

Jennifer stared into the fire, wondering how she could ever tell Peter that she had met another man and fallen in love.

"Here you are, my little lambkins."

"Yes," Jennifer said. "Lambkins: it is until the lambing is over!" She laughed. "All your lovely silly names for me."

"You're mine and mine alone." He sat in the chair opposite her and sipped his own gin and tonic. "I missed you while you were away. It's not the same when you're not here. Poor Chi Chi missed you, too." Chi was sitting by Jennifer's feet with her head resting on her toes. He took another sip. "Do you know that, in the entire twenty-five years we've been married, this is the longest we've been apart? They all missed you - and Bess! Look how happy she was to see you when I brought you back from the station on Friday. She was doing somersaults in the field with joy - we all were!" He got up and walked to the mantelpiece to look at the clock: seven-fifteen. He picked up the little silver plane. "That was very thoughtful, bringing this little feller home from your trip." He put down his empty glass alongside the Jumbo. "I must go and change. Charles will be here soon, dropping Carol off." He leant over and kissed the top of her head. "Cheer up, lambkins - it might never happen."

He went upstairs.

Jennifer stood up with her glass in her hand and moved the plane back to its rightful place. She sat back in her chair, watching the flames dance up the chimney. I must get that piece of paper from my bag before Carol comes. She did say that she would arrange everything. I am so grateful, she thought. We can stay in a little pub or hotel and I can get a taxi to the funeral.

"We're here!"

The taxi pulled to a stop outside the cocktail bar and they got out. 'Copacabana' looked fun - lots of bright lights and Caribbean music coming from inside. Simon opened the door and they walked inside. Jennifer was glad it was warm in there. It had plenty of atmosphere and she loved fun places like this.

A waiter found them a table on the second tier and Simon took Jennifer's wrap and bag from her, placing them on the spare chair at their table. "Now you can relax."

"I'm glad you brought me here," said Jennifer, looking around appreciatively.

"Would you like me to surprise you with your cocktail?"

"Yes! I like surprises."

Simon got up and went to the bar, which was

tucked away behind some huge Caribbean foliage. Jennifer was suddenly aware that he was out of sight and she felt alone. Looking around, she could see there were some drums on a platform by a small dance floor and lots of small tables and chairs. It was still early and she could picture it becoming quite crowded later in the evening. Simon returned. "Did you miss me?" he asked, putting her drink in front of her.

"Yes, I did! Do you come here quite a lot with your wife?"

"No, she wouldn't step foot in a place like this. If I'm staying over in the flat, I come here with friends - various people I've met over the years. I have two lives, really."

Jennifer took a sip of the cocktail. "Ooh, this is nice! What alcoholic concoction is this?"

"Well, you love champagne and fresh oranges… It also has Cointreau and cassis in it."

"It's delicious - and I love this music! It makes me want to dance." Jennifer was already tapping her foot.

"Then, let's dance!" said Simon, standing and offering her his hand.

They walked onto the dance floor hand in hand. He took her in his arms and they smooched. The music was lovely – sultry.

"You're a good dancer," Simon remarked,

admiringly.

"You're so kind," said Jennifer. "I'm hardly moving. We're smooching."

"Well, you're a good smoocher, then!"

Jennifer was enjoying seeing another aspect of him. They had done so much in such a short time.

His head was resting on hers as he thought to himself: oh, my darling Jenny! Did you really think that I could love you just for one day? The music ended.

"That didn't last long."

"No. I was miles away," said Simon.

"So was I," admitted Jennifer. Another song began, more up-tempo this time, and they remained on the dance floor to enjoy themselves.

They eventually returned to their seats. "You were brilliant! Where did you learn to dance?" she asked.

"My mother insisted that we boys had dancing lessons, so we were taught all the social dances, including the samba, the tango and cha cha cha. I hope they play a samba when we go back to the hotel. Can you do the samba?" he asked.

"Yes," said Jennifer. "I had dancing lessons, too."

They sat at their table, enjoying their drinks, whilst watching the other dancers, but the music beckoned them again onto the floor. Simon jived this time, twirling her around. He grabbed her by her waist and pulled her in towards him. She could feel him.

"Is that a pistol in your pocket, or are you just pleased to see me?"

"What do you think?" He kissed her and continued dancing with her whilst his lips remained firmly on hers.

"That was fantastic!" Jennifer said as she sat down. "I haven't danced since Christmas."

"Does Peter dance?"

"Oh, yes. He shuffles a nice shuffle. He used to be a good dancer when we first went out together." She picked up her glass and started to make a funny noise. "Oh, dear! My glass seems to be empty." She sucked through the straw and laughed. Simon shook his head and smiled.

"Should we have another one before we go back to the hotel?"

"That would be lovely. I'm really enjoying myself here," said Jennifer.

"The company's not bad either," said Simon, picking up her glass and giving her a quick kiss as he made his way back to the bar.

Peter entered the room. "Still enjoying your drink, honeybee?"

"Yes. It's lovely sitting by the fire. Lydia loved

curling up by the fire. I can't understand why she loves it so much in Kuwait," she said, trying to cover up how miserable she had been all day.

"Michael's there, my pet, and now Noah."

"Yes, I know."

"Another gin and tonic?"

"No, thank you. Could you please open a bottle of Chablis?"

"Coming up," Peter said, as he left the room.

Jennifer looked at Chi Chi and put down her glass to pick her up. She settled Chi on her lap and stroked her lovely warm coat. Peter returned.

"Thought you might like this." He was carrying an ice bucket with a bottle of champagne in it. "I know how much you love champagne... Charles phoned while I was upstairs. He wants me to meet him at the bottom of the drive."

"I thought I heard the phone," said Jennifer. "Isn't he bringing Carol?"

"She's coming under her own steam, as she had one or two tasks to do. She'll be here about eight-thirty, so that's why I brought these as well," he said, producing a packet of crisps from his jacket pocket. "Can't have you wasting away now, can we?"

"Oh, thank you." She opened the crisps, suddenly realising that she hadn't eaten anything since her breakfast.

"Oh, just before I go: I invited Charles in for a drink after the pub. He said that he'll drive Carol home and she can leave her car here overnight." Peter handed her a glass of champagne and moved the bucket closer to her, so that she could reach it easily. He leant forward and kissed her on her forehead. "Love you. Enjoy your evening. You girls have quite a lot to catch up on."

The front door closed and he was gone. She heard his feet crunch on the gravel as he made his way down the drive. She looked at the wine bucket and her mind wandered back to Simon.

CHAPTER 16

Simon returned, carrying a cooler of champagne. "I thought we might as well start as we mean to go on." He put the cooler on the table. The champagne was already open. "I asked for the cork," he said as he sat down. He opened Jennifer's hand and placed it on her palm, then closed her fingers around it and put his hand on top of hers. "Keep this for always, as a memory of the first time we danced together."

"I will." She leant towards her bag. Simon picked it up and handed it to her. She opened the bag, kissed the cork, dropped it in and closed her bag up, handing it back to Simon. He poured the champagne and offered Jennifer her glass. He picked up his glass. His arm went through Jennifer's and they linked arms and raised their glasses to their lips. He then took Jennifer's glass and exchanged hers for his and then repeated the action again. "I've never done it that way before. Does your wife like champagne?" asked Jennifer.

"No, she doesn't drink. She's a health freak - jogging here, exercising there, organic food whenever she can find it."

"Has she always been like that?"

"No, I don't think so. She's been doing it so long, it's hard to remember. That's why I do the cooking."

"I like good food," said Jennifer, "coming from a farm. We're very lucky and our friends next door have a farm shop. They are arable and we're livestock, but Peter grows food for the animals."

"What animals do you have?"

"We have Hereford cattle. They are so pretty. We have a herd of Friesians, pigs, chickens, ducks on our pond and sheep. I can look out onto one of the fields from my bedroom and see those gorgeous little bundles of white fluff prancing about. Bess, Chi Chi and I go up to the fields where the baby lambs are and welcome them. I hate it when they have to go to market. Occasionally, we have a tiddler lamb and I enjoy looking after them."

Simon listened with interest. "I can understand the name Bess, but why Chi Chi?"

"Oh, Simon, you're not very intelligent, are you?" she laughed. "Black and white Chi Chi panda - London Zoo?"

"I don't care where the name comes from - I just enjoyed watching you explain yourself." He leant towards her, took her by her shoulder and gave her a kiss. Her body started to respond and her mouth accepted his tongue with delight. He held her closely by putting his arms around her back and she put her arms around his neck. "Oh, Jenny, I love you." She leant back in her chair and picked up her champagne. She slipped her left shoe off and stroked his leg with her foot. Simon leant forward and took her foot in both his hands. "You know how I feel. I love you from the top of your head down to your lovely toes."

She sipped her champagne.

"Hello, yoohoo!" called out Carol. "Where are you, Jennifer? Ah, you're sitting in here. I'll put this in the kitchen," she said, holding up a bag of takeaway food.

"Open the Rayburn lower oven and put it in there," Jennifer called from the sitting room.

"Smells delicious. We can enjoy that later," said Carol, sitting down opposite her.

Jennifer handed her a glass of champagne. "Are you feeling a little better?"

"Yes, I do."

"You look better."

"Thank you, Carol, for all you're doing by coming with me. How are we going to tell Charles?"

"Well, I was thinking about that and I sort of felt it out with him this afternoon. I told him that I'd had a phone call from a friend of my godmother," she continued. "She telephoned to tell me that my godmother had died and thought perhaps I would like to know when her funeral was. Oh, Jennifer, you have me lying for you now!"

"I'm so sorry, Carol."

"No, no. I promised I would go with you. Do you have the name of his village, so that I know where the funeral will be?"

"Yes." Jennifer got up from her seat and went into the hall. Her little bag was on one of the hall chairs. She brought it back into the sitting room, opened it and handed Carol the piece of paper. That precious piece of paper, thought Jennifer. Her hand touched the cork. "He gave me this in the nightclub we went to," she said, showing it to Carol. She sat down and kissed the cork. "Oh, why, why? I was going to ring him with my decision this morning."

"And what had you decided?"

"That I was going to stay with Peter. I've lived half my life without Simon. I do love Peter - not in the way that Simon and I loved. We made love, oh, so many times. It was wonderful. I melted every time he touched me. He told me so many things: about him and his life, about his dogs, his wife - he has two sons. He lives in this lovely house. He told me all this over the very short time we had together."

They walked through to the kitchen and Carol got two plates from the cupboard while Jennifer got the food out of the Rayburn. They had finished the champagne. "Let's have a glass of wine," said

Jennifer. She took an already-open bottle of red wine from the dresser, along with two glasses, and they sat down at the kitchen table. Carol dished up their food.

"Cheers! So nice to have you home."

"I feel as though I'm on a gigantic roundabout, whirring around, not knowing which decision to make," said Jennifer. She ate very quickly, realising just how ravenous she was.

"You are hungry!" said Carol. "You've finished before me!" She smiled at her friend. "What made you decide not to leave Peter? You sound as though you've found something that some of us spend all our lives looking for - like me."

"Oh, Carol! You and Charles seem perfect for each other. Appearances deceive. Isn't it funny? If my situation hadn't occurred, we wouldn't be having this conversation."

"So, how could you give up the chance of utter, complete happiness with a man that you obviously loved?"

"Peter and I are cosy with each other. We don't have the same intimacy that Simon and I had - perhaps because we've been together a long time. Simon and I made love on the chair and on the bathroom floor constantly!"

"You're mad, Jennifer. You could have had that all your life!"

"Don't you think that would have faded into the background and, then, what else would Simon and I have?"

"You would have grown old together."

"I don't know, Carol."

"Weren't you going to give yourself a chance to find out?"

"You surprise me, Carol. You, of all people, trying to make me leave the safety of my home."

"You've said it: safety. You were scared. I would jump at the opportunity," said Carol. "Charles is lovely, but he doesn't make me melt. Does Peter?"

"Yes - well, not melt exactly anymore, but, in our younger years…" They both laughed. What an incredible conversation!

"I must go. I told Mother that I would call in and see her. She's not very well - has a cold. I'll tuck her up in bed and make her a warm drink of milk."

"You're so lucky having her still."

"I know. She's a precious lady." Carol got up from her seat and hugged Jennifer. "I'll phone you tomorrow when I've booked us a hotel. Do you mind if I keep this piece of paper with the village name?"

"Sorry, yes I do! I'll write it down for you. That was written by Simon." She looked at his hand writing and started to cry. "I had never seen his writing before. This is now my only connection with him." She wrote down his address and office number and handed it to Carol.

"I've just had a thought," said Carol. "Did you give him your address and telephone number?"

"No, I told him that I'd ring him on Monday morning. I'm glad now, because I would've hated his family to have found anything that would make them suspicious about his trips abroad… But, actually, we do have something else that connects us." Jennifer led Carol into the sitting room and picked up the little Jumbo jet. "This. He bought two." She handed it to Carol.

"What a lovely thing to do!"

"Yes, it was. It was such a lovely day. We rowed on the Serpentine." Jennifer put another log on the fire, hoping that it would come back to life. "Oh, we just had a lovely time." She took back the little Jumbo, kissed it and put it back in its place. She walked her friend to the front door, where Carol kissed Jennifer on the cheek and then departed.

Alone again, Jennifer looked down at Chi Chi, who was at her feet. "Sorry, my petal. I've neglected you for a couple of hours." She picked her up. Goodness! Is that the time? The grandfather clock had chimed ten times. She went back into the sitting room, hoping that the log that she had thrown onto the fire had sparked it back to life. Thankfully, she was greeted by a few flames. She put Chi Chi on the chair, went to the cocktail cabinet and poured herself a Tia Maria. Jennifer then went through to the kitchen, put the kettle on and made herself a cup of coffee. She returned to the sitting room, put her drinks on the table beside her chair, sat down and put Chi Chi on her lap.

"I know I didn't tell Carol the truth and it was very wrong of me. Of course, my darling Simon, I was going to spend the rest of my life with you. We were going to hurt a lot of people, but, as you said, there were only two people in our scenario."

CHAPTER 17

"We're adults. We really are not answerable to anyone." Simon refilled their glasses. Jennifer put her shoe back on.

"I know, Simon, but the fact remains that, for you and me to be together, we do have other things to consider - and an awful lot of people would be hurt."

"I do think about that," said Simon. "I have a conscience as well, but to hell with consciences! We are here once and only once. 'For each is given a bag of tools, an hourglass and a book of rules and each shall have to build, when his hour is flown, a stumbling block or a stepping stone.'"

"What made that come into your mind?" asked Jennifer.

"I don't know. It was written in my autograph book years ago by my ancient aunt's husband, Uncle Cedric."

"It doesn't apply to us though, does it?"

"Yes, it does. Don't you see? The hourglass: that is the time we have left on earth. We have our love, which represents the tools, and, as we grow together, our love will strengthen."

"And the book of rules?" asked Jennifer. "We've already broken one of those."

"Well, two out of three ain't bad," said Simon.

"Don't be so flippant! The commandment: thou shalt not commit adultery… I do understand where you're leading to, Simon. Nothing can ever take this away from us and, if we do decide to leave our spouses… Leave? How can I leave Peter? You're confusing me more and more... I just want the subject to stop. I know, my darling: desperate men do desperate things and, when something as wonderful as you comes into my life - well, we're joined at the hips forever." Jennifer laughed.

"I think that would be just a little too much togetherness." Simon smiled as he handed Jennifer her wrap and bag.

It was a little chilly when they came out of the nightclub. Simon put the wrap around her shoulders. "What are you afraid of, Jenny? Commitment? That I might desert you?"

"I don't want to talk about it."

"You're angry," Simon said. "I didn't mean to make you cross." They started to walk. "If only I'd brought my big coat," said Jennifer.

"You can have my jacket."

"But then you'll be cold."

"I'd much prefer that I was cold than you die of hypothermia. How would I explain that to your family?" He removed his jacket. "Give me your arms." He put her arms in his jacket. It was lovely and warm. He buttoned it up. "Now we will have to snuggle up together." He put his hand in the pocket of the jacket.

"Cuddle me," said Jennifer. They cuddled and started to walk.

"What's the time?"

"Ten-fifteen. Exactly twenty-four hours. It's our anniversary!" Simon exclaimed.

"Twenty-four wonderful hours!"

"Then, why are you so reluctant for us to spend the rest of our lives together? We can't deny ourselves the chance. I know you're happy."

"I am happy."

"I could have gone on the same way for the rest of my life, but the fact is, my darling Jenny, we met twenty-four hours ago and fell in love and I'm not going to give up easily." He stopped and turned her around. "So, my darling, you have a battle on your hands." His lips closed on hers. Oh, it felt lovely and warm in the chill of an April evening. "Even your kisses warm me up." He cuddled up to her again and they continued walking.

"I'm not going to give you my address and telephone number," said Jennifer.

"No, I don't want you to. I want to hear your voice on Monday morning with a decision that I will be eagerly awaiting and, if you decide that we are for keeps, you don't have to go through it on your own. I'll come and stay in Hereford and we can approach Peter together."

"I really don't know that I could be that cruel to Peter. It would devastate him."

"Then, you could tell him yourself."

"No, I don't mean that. I mean I don't know how I could ever leave him."

"So, you would give up a love of the depth of ours?"

"Is it love, Simon? We make love and I love your company. You would lose your house. You might resent me for that in the future."

"Jenny, it's only bricks and mortar and we can have our own home. Do you think that matters to me? I would want my dogs and you could have Bess and your ridiculously named Chi, which I absolutely adore." They had arrived outside The Ritz now.

"Saved by the doorman," said Jennifer, going through the entrance.

"Good evening, sir, madam," said the doorman, with a smile.

"Pleasant evening - bit chilly, though," said Simon, as he followed Jennifer into the hotel, shuddering as he did.

"Oh, my darling! I have your jacket." She removed it and gave it back to him. "Do you still want to go through to the dining room? The music sounds very inviting."

"Should I see if we can get some supper?" They approached the dining room. "Are we still all right for supper?" Simon asked a waiter.

"Yes, sir. Would you like a table?"

"Thank you." Simon took Jennifer's hand and followed the waiter, who found them a table in a cosy spot. "Would you like the wine list?

"Should we stick to champagne?" he asked, turning to Jennifer.

"Darling, yes, please."

"Moët, please."

"I'm going to powder my nose," said Jennifer. She got up from her seat and, as she did so, he grabbed her hand.

"I'm sorry. I didn't mean to bully you."

"I know." She smiled back at him. "I won't be long."

The waiter returned with the champagne. "Would you like me to open it now, before your wife returns?"

"Yes, please."

The waiter put the cork on the table and Simon picked it up. It was in his hand when Jennifer returned.

"I feel much better now." She was carrying her wrap and had replenished her make-up and sprinkled a little perfume on the appropriate places.

Simon stood up as she approached, taking her wrap and bag and putting them on top of his jacket on the spare chair at their table. He put the cork in his jacket pocket. She sat next to him and glanced around the room.

"You are a beautiful lady." He handed her glass of champagne to her. She sipped it and then put it in front of him. Simon returned the favour.

"Aren't we silly? We do daft things - things that people years younger do. We're oblivious to anything going on around us. It's like being in a bubble - we're the only people in the world. Whoops! I think all the lovely drink we've had this evening is going to my head. I feel quite dizzy! Let's order some food." Simon called over a waiter and asked for a menu. Jennifer yawned.

"You're tired, my darling."

"I've never done so much in such a short time. Twenty-four hours."

Simon nodded. "One day in our lives. Not long, is it?"

"No, it isn't," agreed Jennifer, "but how can we throw our lives away for one happy day?"

"We wouldn't be throwing our lives away. We would keep our lives, but we would live them together." Simon touched her hand. "Now, my darling: food."

"I'll eat anything," said Jennifer.

Simon called over the waiter and ordered two Spanish omelettes and a salad to share. He poured Jennifer another glass of champagne and leant towards her. Taking her hands and holding them gently, he said, "This time yesterday, we had only just met and I knew as soon as I saw you that I was going to spend the rest of my life with you." Jennifer moved closer to him and kissed him on the cheek. The music started again. "Let's dance," he said and they got up and walked hand in hand to the dance floor.

CHAPTER 18

The men had returned from the pub. Jennifer had hoped to be in bed by the time they came back. She walked into the kitchen.

"Hello, my dear. Did you have a nice evening with Carol?"

"Yes, thank you. Where's Charles? I thought he was coming in?"

"No. He saw that Carol's car was gone, so he decided to go home. He sent this:" and he kissed her on her cheek. "I'll go and secure the doors and switch the lights off. Okay, lambkins?"

She went upstairs, took a nightie out of the drawers in her bathroom and put it on. Peter came upstairs a few minutes later and went into his bathroom to prepare for bed. Ablutions complete, Jennifer switched off her bathroom light and walked into the bedroom just as Peter was getting into bed. "What do you need that on for?" he asked, pointing to her nightie.

"I wanted to wear it. I feel cold."

"Come here, my darling. I'll warm you up." She did as he asked and removed it, climbed into bed and put her head on the pillow. Peter switched off his bedside lamp. It was dark and Jennifer knew what was coming. Peter moved closer. He raised his body between her legs under the covers. He bit her nipple.

"Ouch, that hurt!"

"Sorry, my pet."

"Do it gently. Just kiss them."

His large hand came up to the other nipple and rolled her breast under his palm, his other hand supporting his weight. He removed his hand from her breast and placed it between her legs. He then shoved his fingers into her vagina and moved his fingers in and out. He grabbed hold of her hand and made her grab his penis. With his hand on top of hers, he rubbed it up and down. He removed his hand and lifted himself up into position to enter her, then thrust himself inside her. Just like one of his farm animals, she thought. His stomach rested on her tummy and he groaned as he came. Silent tears started to roll down the side of Jennifer's face into her hair. She was so glad that he could not see her tears. He slipped out of her, dangling over her legs as he went back to his side of the bed. "We should do that more often!" he said. "You forget how good it is."

He was fast asleep soon afterwards, snoring like an old bull. Jennifer got out of bed and went into the bathroom. She sat on the bidet and turned on the taps. The tears started to flow. "Oh, my darling Simon. Why didn't I give you my answer?" She turned on the douche and directed the flowing water. She pulled out the plug so that she could masturbate with the help of the surging water. She aimed the flow towards her clitoris and closed her eyes. The water made her throb and her vagina swell. She was ready to make love. Oh, Simon, why did you have to die? She climaxed again and again, moving her body with the spurts of water. She gradually stopped moving and turned off the douche, raised herself up from the bidet, dried herself and put on her silk dressing robe.

She decided to sleep in the guest room. Peter snored so much. She knew he would understand. She went along the landing to the guest room, opened the door, walked over to the table by the bed and switched on the small lamp. The bed looked very inviting. She turned back the covers and slid down into the virgin clean sheets. She reached over to turn off the lamp. Now it was dark, the moon was peeping through the window.

He swung her around and around to the music, lifting her off her feet, and then, pulling her closer, he whispered in her ear, "I will always love you." She hugged him, their bodies close. She could feel his body through his shirt, which was damp from dancing, and rubbed her hands up and down his back. They slowed down and smooched and stayed this way for the rest of the dance, her head on his chest and his head buried in her hair. When the song finished, they returned, hand in hand, to their table, where their food was served. They ate their supper, chatting away, oblivious to anyone around them.

"That was lovely," said Jennifer. "I'm ready for anything."

"Anything?" asked Simon, raising an eyebrow.

"I would like to go to our room."

Simon called for the bill and signed it off. Jennifer thought his signature was extremely distinguished. "Good night, Mr and Mrs Green." They were getting used to that name.

Simon opened the door to their room. The lights were already on and the bed had been turned down. Jennifer sat on the bed. Simon was already removing his tie as he sat down on the edge of the bed. He turned around and unzipped her dress. Jennifer stood up and stepped out of it, kicking it across the room. Totally out of character, she stood in front of Simon and started to undo her suspenders. He removed his shirt rapidly and threw it towards Jennifer's dress. He moved closer, rolled down one of her stockings and took it off. She sat down on the bed. He did the same with the other stocking. Simon knelt on the floor and slowly removed her panties and her suspender belt, tossing it over his shoulder. She moved her body towards him, so that she could put her legs round his neck. He moved her eager body nearer his waiting lips. He could smell their love from earlier. He nuzzled his mouth into her pubic hair and let his tongue move where it wanted to. "Yes, yes, oh, yes!" She climaxed in his mouth. He drank in her sigh. She was moving to the rhythm of his tongue. "Oh, Simon! Never, never stop!"

He emerged from this other-worldly experience and Jennifer released her hold on his neck. He stood up and removed his trousers and pants as she removed her bra. He lay her back on the bed and entered her. He moved with great confidence and she immediately responded likewise. Their kisses were urgent, but sensual. He gently withdrew. "Have you come yet?" she asked.

"No, I want it to last," he murmured, as he kissed her again, moving on to her neck and her ear lobes. His hand went towards the part that had been awakened earlier and rubbed her clitoris with knowledge. His mouth went to her right nipple, biting it gently and rolling it between his teeth, then using his tongue to toy with it. He did the same with the other nipple. Her hand found his magnificent penis. It was throbbing between her fingers. She guided it towards her welcoming entrance. He moved quite slowly, repeatedly withdrawing and then entering and going a little bit further each time. He kissed her lips and moved a little higher and then withdrew once more. Then he went all the way in. She climaxed immediately, moaning loudly. He exploded with absolute delight.

He lay gently on top of her. They were both totally exhausted. He lifted his head from her breast and looked up at her face. "The greatest gift in life is love and to be loved in return." He then lifted himself off Jennifer and stood, fondly looking down at her. Jennifer stayed where she was, thinking about the words that he had just said. He bent down towards her, took her hands in his, pulled her up and held her. "Do you agree?" he asked. She nodded.

A short while later, when they had both finished in the bathroom, Jennifer slid into the bed beside him. He welcomed her with his open arms and she cuddled up into his shoulder. They lay together on the pillows and Simon kissed her head. "What are we going to do tomorrow?" he asked. She looked up at him and he kissed her on her lips. The look in her eyes told him what she wanted to do. Simon turned off the lights and pulled Jennifer towards him. His arm remained around her waist as they fell asleep.

CHAPTER 19

"Mrs Darling, Mrs Darling! Mr Peter asked me to bring up your breakfast on a tray. He said you were feeling a bit poorly."

"Oh, thank you, Mrs Thompson." Jennifer's eyes were quite sticky from sleeping, so she wiped them with her sleeve. "Could you please get my tissues from the bathroom?" Mrs Thompson placed the tray on the table close to Jennifer, fetched the tissues and returned with them. "Thank you. I was so sorry to hear about your aunt. She was a grand age."

"My mother's eldest sister."

Jennifer sat up in bed and Mrs Thompson handed her the tray. "Boiled eggs and soldiers. Just how you like it - and wholemeal bread, too."

"Oh, lovely! Thank you." She picked up her fresh orange juice and sipped it. Mrs Thompson poured her a cup of coffee.

"Now, you stay there as long as you like. It's my day for changing the beds, anyway, and I'll start in yours and Mr Peter's room."

Mrs Thompson left and closed the door. Jennifer tucked into her breakfast, spreading copious amounts of Marmite on her toast. Vitamin B is good for you when under stress, dear Mummy used to say. Once finished, she put the tray on the table, got out of bed and called to Mrs Thompson as she went into the bathroom. "Bedroom's free...and thank you for my breakfast."

She put plenty of smellies under the flow of water, dropped her robe to the floor and stepped into the warm, inviting bath. She sunk herself deep into the bubbles, right up to her neck, closed her eyes and soaked up the soothing aroma.

Jennifer was awakened by Simon behind her, his arousal resting between her legs. He was moving slowly so that Jennifer was aware of his request. She parted her legs slightly and he pulled her bottom towards his loins, where she was met with the part of his body that she was thinking she couldn't live without. His hand wandered over her legs and rested on her already moist mound. His fingers stroked her pubic hair and moved around freely. Oh, how she loved the way he touched her! He pushed the pillows off the bed, gently splayed her legs and lay between them. Kissing her back with his soft lips, he lowered himself towards her bottom. She opened her legs a little further, he wiggled himself into position and slid into her ever-inviting body. He put his arm around her waist so that he could penetrate deeper. His other hand went under her tummy and between her legs and rubbed her clitoris vigorously. He was moving with so much energy! It was exquisite, Jennifer thought. Her legs widened and he went deeper. Jennifer climaxed again and again. She lay in his arms afterwards, "Oh, Simon, that was wonderful."

"Yes, it was wonderful," Simon agreed, as he raised his head to face Jennifer. "Jenny, Jenny, how wonderful our lives could be."

"I know," said Jennifer. "I'm beginning to think that I do want to spend the rest of my life with you and your dogs and sons."

Simon got off the bed and put on his towelling robe. "They would love you almost as much as I do." He held up her robe and she got off the bed. Simon held it out, slipped it over her body and they both sat back down on the bed.

"But, Simon, how can we have fallen in love in such a short time?" She went over to his watch, picked it up. The time was exactly eight-fifteen.

"Look, Simon! Look at the time!" She showed him the watch. "It's nearly thirty-six hours since our first meeting. How can a couple, who have just met, fall in love and want to spend the rest of their lives together? It's not possible!"

"Yes, it is!" He looked up at her, took her by her hands and sat her down on the bed next to him. "Look what happened in the war. Couples met, fell in love, married - all in thirty-six hours."

"Yes," said Jennifer, "but there was a strong

possibility they would never see each other again."

"Are we going to see each other again?" asked Simon.

"I don't know." She rose and went into the bathroom. Simon heard the water running. He walked in after her, knowing that she was trying to avoid him.

"You're crying."

"No, I'm not."

"Yes, you are," he said softly, as he turned her towards him. Her face was wet.

"What's that then? Moisture from the steam of the bath?" She laughed. "That's better."

She removed her robe and stepped into the warm soapy water, followed by Simon. "Jenny, my dearest. Just suppose we were in a similar position to those lovers in the war and had met as we did."

"Not on a Jumbo," said Jennifer. "By the way, where are our planes?"

"In my sports jacket pocket. Now, stop changing the subject. I'm trying to find something out here," said Simon.

"Sorry." She leant towards him. "I'll be a very attentive little girl from now on."

"Thank you." He continued. "And if we had met, would you have left me today, never to see me again?"

"No," said Jennifer. "I would have married you

in a flash."

He leant back. "Then, what's the difference?"

"Ah," said Jennifer, "they were going to war."

"There are no comparisons with love, Jenny. You either are in love or you're not. Those soldiers returned and continued their lives. They always loved their wives. The fact remains that it all happened on their first meeting." Jennifer turned around and Simon picked up the sponge and started to wash her back. "I won't easily let you turn me down," he said. "I want to know if we have a future. I need to know."

Jennifer turned back to face him. "All we have had is a hotel room for thirty-six hours. We've made love many times and it's been wonderful. I think that I really love you, but Peter has provided me with a lovely, secure lifestyle with no worries. There's no excitement, as I've told you, but I have everything I need."

"Except love," said Simon.

"Yes, I do."

"Has he ever done the things that we do?"

"Have you done the things that we do with your wife?"

"We've made love, obviously. We have two sons, but I can honestly say that I have never needed her body like I need yours. You are nectar to my soul." He put her hand on his chest. "Feel my heart." It was beating under her hand. Oh, how she loved his heart!

"Mrs Darling?"
"Uh, yes, Mrs Thompson?"
"I'm going downstairs to make myself a cup of coffee. I've finished up here apart from the bathroom."

"Thank you, Mrs Thompson. I'll be down in a jiff." The water was quite chilly now, and the bubbles had all dispersed. Jennifer climbed out of the bath, rushed into the bedroom and got dressed hurriedly, throwing on a pair of jeans and a sweater. When she arrived downstairs, a mug of coffee was waiting for her on the kitchen table. She sat in the chair by the Rayburn.

"You're always such a friendly, warm welcome, Mrs Thompson."

"That's just what my Frank says when he comes home at night. He enjoys working for Mr Peter. And we liked the old boss - he were a proper gentleman - and Mrs Darling senior. Frank retires next year. Yes, we are ever so grateful that he would allow my Frank and me to live in the cottage for the rest of our days."

"Well, that's what you get for loyalty," replied Jennifer warmly, as she put down her mug, got up and walked towards the back door. She put on her riding boots and took her coat off the back door hook. "Chi Chi, come."

"She's with my Frank. Going to ride Bess, are you?"

"Yes."

"They missed you while you were away. My Frank swore that he could hear her crying in her stable."

"See you tomorrow, Mrs Thompson. I won't be here Friday, though. That's my aunt's funeral." Jennifer closed the door behind her and walked towards the stable. Her aunt's funeral, not darling Simon's.

She looked into the field and saw Bess grazing on the sweet-smelling summer grass. "Hello, my lovely." Bess lifted her head. "Do you want to go for a walk?" Jennifer called. Bess came rushing towards her and Jennifer greeted her by holding her lovely velvety nose in her hands and kissing it. "Do you want to go for a walk?" She looked into her eyes and Bess followed her into the stable. Jennifer put her saddle on and gently secured it underneath. She went outside into the yard with Bess following. She put her boot into the stirrup, swung herself up and mounted. They were making their way out of the yard when Jennifer spotted Frank. "Hello, Frank, could you please clean Bess's stable for her?"

"Mr Peter has already asked me, Mrs Darling."

"Where is my husband?"

"It's market day."

"Oh, yes, of course it is! You forget these things when you go away. Walk on!" Bess dutifully obeyed and, just as they were about to leave the yard, Chi Chi came rushing towards her. "Do you want to go for your walk as well, Chi?" She barked in reply and Jennifer laughed. The trio climbed the small hill and went into the little copse, where the bluebells were coming into flower and the aconites and primroses were like a golden carpet stretching out in front of them. Jennifer dismounted to allow Bess to have a browse.

"Mrs Darling!" Jennifer turned around. It was Frank, who was a little puffed. "Mrs Darling! Thank goodness I caught you! Phew! That's quite a hill! My missus has made a flask of hot chocolate for you." He handed Jennifer the flask.

"Thank you, Frank! I was just thinking how lovely it would be to have a hot drink! Do thank Margaret for me."

Frank made his way back down the hill as Jennifer enjoyed her surprise hot chocolate and took in the lovely view over the fields. She admired the violet-blue of the bluebells close by and the sweet-scented primroses under the trees. Bess had found some lovely fresh grass to munch on – so much more enjoyable without her bit, thought Jennifer. Chi was nestled beside her on the ground. Jennifer called over to Bess. Bess moved closer, but not too close, as she had found some lovely fresh grass and was keeping her nose firmly stuck to the ground. Her ears moved with the sound of Jennifer's voice and her eyes glanced in Jennifer's direction. Jennifer knew how much Bess loved her. Chi was in her favourite position, lying on her back, so that she could have her tummy rubbed. Jennifer could feel Chi's heart beating under her hand.

CHAPTER 20

She took her hand off his soft, curly chest hair. "I have a train to catch." Jennifer got out of the bath, took a warm towel from the rail and handed another to Simon. She pulled hers around her. "I think I ought to make a phone call to the farm and tell Mrs Thompson to let Peter know what time I'll be arriving at the station."

"Who's Mrs Thompson?" Simon enquired.

"She's my help. She and her husband live in a tied cottage on our estate." Jennifer picked up the phone. "Hello. This is room twenty-four. Please may I have an outside line?" She sat on the edge of the bed, while Simon crawled onto the bed and knelt behind her, putting his arms around her waist. Jennifer dialled her home number, then listened until the phone was picked up, dreading that it would be Peter - especially with these lovely silky arms around her waist.

"Hello, Mrs Thompson. It's Mrs Darling here… Yes, I had a lovely time, thank you. Yes, the baby is fine. Yes, yes, the reason I'm phoning, Mrs Thompson, is to say that I'll be leaving here on the two o'clock train from Paddington. Will you please make sure that Mr Peter is there to meet me?" Simon's grip tightened around her waist. "Oh, he said so this morning? Ah, okay. I'll see you on Monday. Goodbye." She replaced the receiver.

"What was all that about?" asked Simon. She turned towards him.

"Peter had already said that he was meeting me from the train and could she light a fire in the sitting room and rustle up a casserole for our supper."

"She sounds wonderful! I could do with one of those at my home! Do you think she would come and live with us in our little cottage in the countryside?"

"You don't get me that easily, sweet Simon." She kissed his forehead and went into the bathroom. Simon went over to his suitcase and removed a few items - the clothes that he would travel home in. He took his sports jacket from the wardrobe and quickly felt in the pocket. There they were in their identical boxes. He placed them side by side on the chair, whilst thinking about some kind of commemorative handing-over for when he gave Jennifer hers. He picked up his clothes from the frenzy of the night before, felt the pocket of his suit jacket and retrieved the cork. He had meant to ask Jennifer to write something on his, and he would do so on hers. He put the cork by the side of the little parcels just as Jennifer came through the door. She walked towards him. "Simon, my lovely Simon, we have very little time left before we have to part.

Let's make the most of it."

"No, I'm going to stay here for the rest of my life!" He was lying rigidly on the bed.

"No, you're not! You're going to get off that bed and we're going to have a lovely morning together." She was trying to pull him off the bed.

"I'll only get off if you promise me that you'll ring me on Monday morning when I'm at my office."

"Yes, yes, I promise I'll phone you on Monday morning and we'll have a lovely chat on the phone."

"You'll have a decision for me?"

"I'll not promise that, but I assure you, my darling Simon, that this is not the end. Now get off that bed!"

He jumped off the bed. "You mean that we're going to see each other again and this isn't the end?" He grabbed her and held her tightly to his body. "Oh, Jenny, Jenny! You've made me the happiest man alive." He twirled her around and around. "Let's quickly get dressed and enjoy the rest of the day." He skipped into the bathroom and started singing whilst he was shaving: 'I'm getting married in the morning, ding dong the bells are gonna to chime'.

Simon got dressed very quickly. He was sitting on the chair, putting on his shoes, when Jennifer returned. She took off her robe and removed her clothes from her large suitcase. She decided that she would wear the clothes that she was wearing when they first met. She took her suit and silk shirt out of the wardrobe and Simon watched her get dressed. She went back into the bathroom and closed the door. Simon was amused by her little moment of insecurity. She emerged after a while with her hair done and her make-up freshly applied. A quick squirt of perfume, her pearl necklace on and she was done. Simon came over to her. "I've been watching you." He put his arms around her waist and turned her towards him.

"Bess, your nose is cold. Bess, stop it!" Bess was nudging Jennifer with her nose. "I know you're telling me you want to continue our walk." Jennifer picked up Chi and held her under her arm whilst she mounted Bess and then draped Chi across the saddle and watched as Chi made herself comfortable. Bess started to walk on through the copse. The air was warming, so Jennifer removed her coat and tied it around her waist, trying not to disturb Chi. It was good to be out in the early summer air. She looked all around their land, with the cattle in the far field and the old Hereford bull. It reminded her of Peter last night. He had always made Jennifer content, because she didn't have anybody to compare him with - not until that dratted Simon. Why, oh, why, did he have to be on my flight and why did Liddy have to point him out at the airport and why the hell did we have to fall for each other? Bess was waddling up the hill, putting her head down from time to time, having a nibble of the newly grown grass. Chi was quite happy being cuddled. They came to the top of the hill and Jennifer took in the lovely view. She could see the daffodils in front of the house, which were nearly over, and Frank and Tom going about their farm duties. "I think we'll make our way back now, girls." Bess turned around and Jennifer patted her on her neck. "You know exactly what I'm thinking, don't you?"

"You know exactly what I'm thinking, don't you?" Simon said to Jennifer.

"I have a pretty good idea," she replied, "and those are my thoughts as well, but we don't have much more time together." She removed his arms and went to her cases. "What are we going to do with our luggage?"

"I could ask reception if they have a room where we can leave our luggage, so that we can change and refresh for your journey back to Hereford," Simon suggested.

"Yes, that's a good idea."

"Right, then. I'll go and pay our bill and make enquiries." He kissed Jennifer on the cheek, closed the door and was gone. The room suddenly seemed so quiet and empty. This is what it's going to be like in a few hours, Jennifer thought sadly. He won't be close to me and, when I'm on the train this afternoon, each mile will take me further and further away from him.

Bess came to an abrupt stop. "You should warn Chi and me that you've found something nice to munch on!" Holding Chi tightly, Jennifer dismounted and then put Chi on the ground. Chi gave herself a huge shake, which nearly made her fall over. Jennifer laughed. She started to walk down the hill towards the farmyard. Chi was at her heels and Bess followed. "Come, Bess! I'll put you in here. You like the top field, don't you?" Jennifer opened the gate, removed the saddle and Bess cantered off down the field. Jennifer draped the saddle over the fence. "Enjoy it, my lovely! I'll be back later. Come, Chi." She walked further down, towards the farmyard. Once in the yard, she could see that Peter had returned from market.

"Hello, pigeon." Peter put his arm around her and kissed her on the cheek. "Did you enjoy your lie-in?" he asked. "Would you like me to light a fire for you? Then you and Chi can curl up with a good book."

"I'll be all right, thank you. I thought I'd go into town and do some shopping. I won't be long." She kissed Peter on the cheek.

"You're looking more like your old self. It must have been last night that did it," said Peter and he tapped her bottom.

Jennifer walked into the house. Mrs Thompson was in the kitchen. "I've made you some of them sandwiches that you like. I thought that Mr Peter was at the market."

"Yes, so did I. I forgot to ask him why he was back so early," said Jennifer.

"Anyway, I've put some of that clingy stuff over them."

"Thank you, Mrs Thompson." Jennifer went over to Chi Chi's bowl and filled it with fresh water. "I'm going upstairs and then I'm going into town. Is there anything you would like me to get for you, Mrs Thompson?"

"I'd like you to get me one of them bereavement cards you give when somebody dies, with you having good taste. You can choose much better than me."

"All right. I'll buy you a bereavement card, a nice one with flowers on, perhaps."

"I can collect it tomorrow when I comes to work, okay?"

Jennifer went upstairs and into the bedroom. It smelt really fresh, just like spring flowers, and there, on the small table by the bed, was a little display of flowers from the garden. "Mrs Thompson, are you still there?" she called.

"Yes, just leaving now."

"Thank you for my flowers."

"I thought you might like them. Cheer you up a bit."

"Yes, thank you. They are a lovely surprise." She went towards her suitcases. She had not even unpacked yet. There they were, stacked neatly on the sofa by the window. She lifted the two small ones onto the floor. The middle case she put by the side of the wardrobe, so that she could hang her clothes up later. She opened her little vanity case and there it was: the small spray of flowers, wrapped lovingly in a tissue for its journey home. She picked it up. It had been there since Friday.

CHAPTER 21

"Hello! Did you miss me?" asked Simon.
"Of course I did."
"Aren't you going to ask me what I have behind my back?"
Jennifer obliged. "What do you have behind your back?" Simon produced a lovely little scented spray of flowers.

She put her nose towards it. It still had a wonderful scent. She held it gently in her hands, went to her bathroom and took a glass from the cupboard. She unwrapped it and put it in the glass. She had had every intention of pressing the flowers, so she could show Simon one day. She carried the posy back to her bedroom and placed it on her dressing table.

"Oh, Simon! How lovely! How thoughtful! My favourites! How did you know? Lily of the valley, violets and the tiniest narcissi!" She was thrilled. "Thank you, oh, thank you!" She put her arms around his neck carefully so as not to disturb the flowers. He kissed her.

"There's no issue with the luggage. We can have it transferred to another room."

Jennifer went to her small vanity case and pulled out several pieces of tissue paper. "I'll wrap these very gently. It's a pity we're not staying another night, as I would be able to get the full benefit of their loveliness."

"We can! I don't always go home on a Friday evening. Could we stay another night, please?"

"No," said Jennifer. "Of course I want to stay here with you - anywhere with you - but I must go home and do a lot of thinking about us." She placed the flowers carefully into her vanity case.

There was a knock on the door. It was the porter to collect their luggage. "The vacant room for your bags is just down the hall, sir. Room twenty-nine." The porter piled their cases onto a trolley and closed the door. Simon and Jennifer took one last look around the room.

"Bye, room." Jennifer sat on the bed. "Bye, lovely room and lovely bed."

"Come on, you old romantic."

Jennifer went back to the bathroom. She had a quick freshen-up and returned to the bedroom, brushed her hair, put a little make-up on and pulled out a clean pair of jeans from the wardrobe. She went downstairs into the hall, picked up her bag and opened it as she walked through to the kitchen and collected her car keys from the hook. "Are you coming, Chi?" She reached into her handbag to get her car keys, her fingers briefly touching the champagne cork. Chi Chi walked along dutifully by her side as they headed to the car. And off they went down the drive. The trees either side were in bud and leafing, and primroses dotted the verges all the way to the main road.

As they entered town, Jennifer remembered it was market day. "Look, Chi! There's Teddy." She pulled up and wound down her window. "Hello, Teddy."

"Nice to see you, Mrs Darling. Do you need somewhere to park?"

"I do. Can I park here, please?"

"Yes, the market is practically finished now."

"Thanks, Ted," she smiled.

"Would you like me to take Chi for a walk?" he asked.

"No, I won't be too long, but thank you."

"How's Lydia?"

"She's fine, Ted. I know how very fond you are of her."

"I always thought that we would get married. So did Mum and Dad, being adjacent farmers' children growing up together."

"It was not to be Ted, I know."

She reversed into a space with Teddy's help. Jennifer turned to Chi. "You stay here. I won't be long." She left the windows slightly open for her.

Jennifer and Simon were standing outside the hotel.

"Where should we go?"

"I'd like to go to that little café by the Serpentine - the one you pointed out yesterday." He took hold of her hand as they walked into the park. It was a lovely spring morning and they headed to the river just in front of them.

"Would you like to go rowing again?" Simon asked.

"I did enjoy it," replied Jennifer. "Let's see how the time goes."

"Ah, here's the restaurant."

They sat down at a table with a nice view of the park, people on bicycles and people hand in hand, walking their dogs. Jennifer's thoughts were miles away. Simon moved closer. "What's the matter? You don't seem to be part of this earth?"

"I was just looking at that couple walking their dog."

"Which couple?"

She pointed. "There!" An elderly couple was walking towards them.

"Yes. Do you think they met and fell in love as quickly as we did?"

"They look very happy."

The lady and gentleman were approaching the restaurant. The lady smiled at Jennifer.

"I think she knows," said Jennifer.

"Knows what?"

"That we love each other. She gave me a lovely warm smile."

Simon smiled and started to look at the menu. "Breakfast. What should we have for breakfast?" It wasn't long before the waitress appeared at their table, notepad at the ready.

"A large pot of tea, toasted teacakes and honey, please," said Jennifer. "Oh, and two fresh orange juices." Simon nodded in agreement.

Once the waitress had departed with their order, Simon moved his chair closer to Jennifer's and held her hands. "Tell me more about Lydia. Why did she go to live in Kuwait, which I know you hate?"

"Lydia met Michael at university. She was training to be a midwife and Michael a doctor. After they had qualified, the opportunity for them both to work in Kuwait came up and they discussed it with Peter and me. Obviously, I was devastated. She had never been away to school - she wanted to stay home with us. She did jolly well at the local girls' school, too, and got all the relevant qualifications for her chosen career. She loves it in Kuwait and now, of course, has dear little Noah, but she really misses all the family get-togethers."

The waitress brought their breakfast and placed it all out on the table.

"I'll pour," said Simon.

Whilst they were tucking into their delicious breakfast, Jennifer took a sip of her tea, leant back in her chair and said, "Oh, Simon, what are we going to do?"

"What do you mean, what are we going to do? We are going to do exactly what that lovely elderly couple were doing just a little while ago. We are going to enjoy the rest of our lives together. Become a real Darby and Joan." Jennifer laughed. "You Joan, me Darby. I once read (or was I told?) that you only really, truly fall in love once in your life and you should seize the opportunity if ever it comes your way."

"You've just made that up," said Jennifer.

"I know, but it sounded good though, didn't it?"

"I know what you mean, my darling Simon, and I have promised to phone you on Monday morning, haven't I? Neither of us expected this to happen: a chance meeting on a plane; to fall in love and to disrupt and change our lives forever; for you to hurt your wife, I have no doubt, and for me to destroy Peter - I know that will be the effect." She sighed. "I am his life, but, since Liddy has been away, we've grown apart – we're more like a comfy pair of slippers by the fire."

CHAPTER 22

Jennifer walked through the back door into the kitchen, followed by Chi Chi. She put her basket of shopping on the kitchen table, took the bereavement card, which she had bought for Mrs Thompson, out of her bag and put it on the dresser. She took the neatly wrapped sandwiches out of the fridge and put the kettle on to make herself a nice pot of tea. She then carried the tray into the sitting room, where the fire had been lit, settled down in her chair and poured out her tea. Chi was by her side. "I know you want some of my sandwich to fall at your feet," said Jennifer, smiling.

Simon poured Jennifer another cup of tea. It was a bit cold and strong for Jennifer's taste. "Can we pay our bill? We don't have much time before I must go to catch my train." She sighed. "We are so lucky to have found each other, Simon, but I'm very concerned about the hurt that our love is going to cause so many people."

"We wouldn't be caring people if we didn't have those concerns," replied Simon, "and I'm guessing that you really wish we'd never met and that you were now already back in Hereford. But we did. Are you regretting our meeting?" he asked, nudging

Jennifer. "No, it's because we're about to part and you're going back to Peter, isn't it?"

"Yes. This reminds me of Brief Encounter - but nowadays," said Jennifer. "I don't suppose they made love."

"I think they did," said Simon. "He borrowed a colleague's flat and they went for a ride in his car on several occasions. The only reason they split up was because he went to Africa."

"No, I disagree. She finished it because her husband and her children loved her so much. Do you think, if it had been now, she would've gone to Africa with him?"

"I think she would have."

"Probably so," agreed Jennifer.

Simon smiled. "Just like us, my darling." He kissed her on her cheek and went to the counter to pay the bill.

They then walked into the sunshine and made their way towards the Serpentine, not saying a word. They strolled quite slowly this time, not in the enthusiastic way they had walked yesterday. "You're very quiet," observed Simon.

"I was just thinking," replied Jennifer. "This time yesterday, we were starting our time together - and now it's a couple of hours until we part until who knows when?"

"It will be soon," said Simon. "I'll try to get

down the week after next. Is it possible for us to spend some time together then?"

"Yes," she said, linking her arm into Simon's.

"I'll book into a small hotel not too far from your village," said Simon, as they sat down on a bench. The elderly couple they had seen earlier were arm in arm in the distance. Simon took hold of Jennifer's hand. "We can have some special time together and get to know more about each other." He laid her hand on his lap and pulled her closer. Putting his arm around her shoulder, he pulled her close and kissed her mouth with a passionate longing. He held onto her lips as if he never wanted to let go. She loved his kisses. "Oh, Jenny! I'm going to miss you so much."

"Hello, cherub. You haven't touched your sandwiches."

"I must have drifted off. It's so lovely and warm by the fire and Chi is like a hot water bottle by my feet."

"I've just put the kettle on. Would you like a cuppa?"

"Yes, that would be lovely, thank you."

Peter took the tray away into the kitchen and Jennifer got up and put another log on the fire with a sprinkling of coal. Peter returned with a tray of tea.

"Tom and I have volunteered to sleep over at the barn tonight. I don't suppose we'll get much sleep, though, as there are a few ewes causing some concern."

"Why do you have to do this, Peter? It's not as if we're in need of all this commitment. We're not exactly poor church mice." Peter handed Jennifer a cup of tea.

"I know. But it's the family farm - my birth obligation."

"Birth obligation! Phooey! We never do anything together. You won't come on holiday. You don't even go to Kuwait with me." She was wishing that he had and then the situation that was now brewing would not be taking place. "I want to travel and see the world," said Jennifer.

"Is this what the matter's been since you came home? You've been so restless."

"I hate Liddy being so far away and this trip has made me realise that, after the christening and their return to Kuwait, they might not come home so often and, then, what have we got?"

Peter walked over to her and sat on the arm of her chair. "We have each other, my pet. You and I, growing old together." Jennifer started to cry. "Oh, no, my love. It's nothing to cry about. We have the security for our old age. There won't be any money problems and we'll always have a roof over our heads. We should count our blessings."

"But where's the excitement, Peter? What fun will we have?"

Peter returned to his chair - always opposite her, by the fireplace. They were like two bookends, thought Jennifer. "You've always seemed content. You've never queried anything before. What happened to you in Kuwait, Jennifer?"

"Nothing." It's what happened to me in London, she thought.

"You must have caught sun stroke, or one of those foreign viruses."

Jennifer got up from her seat. She could not suppress her feelings any longer. "No, Peter. Realisation. I realised, whilst I was away, that I love you, but I am not in love with you."

"What was that last night? Wasn't that love?"

"Yes, that was your love, Peter, not mine."

She walked through to the kitchen. Peter followed silently, dazed and in a state of shock, placed the tray on the draining board and walked out through the back door. Damn, she thought, as she poked the dying embers in the Rayburn. She dropped into her chair and burst into tears, ashamed of the way she had just treated him. Oh, Simon, Simon! You made me say all those horrid things to Peter. All the plans that we were going to make for our future life together, then you died. You died and you can no longer feel the things I feel, but, because of you, I've hurt Peter dreadfully. I'll be glad when Friday is over, so that I can come back to the life I know and love.

They were on the lake again and Simon was rowing. "Thank you for suggesting this," said Jennifer happily, as she trailed her hand in the water and splashed Simon as she watched him row. She stretched her legs towards him and touched his knee with her shoe.

"Can I row?" she asked.

"Yes, I'll come over to you and sit by your side. You can have one oar and I'll have the other." He tentatively made his way towards Jennifer and sat by her side, to her left. He placed the oar in the righthand rowlock for Jennifer and handed it to her. "It's easier for you to row with your right hand," he explained.

"Thank you. You're always so thoughtful."

They were rowing in unison and Jennifer was trying to keep up with Simon. The family of ducks they saw yesterday swam by. "Mum's not grumpy like she was yesterday," observed Jennifer.

"She's clearly impressed with our rowing!" joked Simon. Jennifer laughed, watching the baby ducks quack as they swam past.

"I love your laughter," said Simon. Jennifer

turned towards him and gave him a kiss. "Oh, how much I love you!"

Looking into Simon's irresistible eyes, Jennifer pleaded, "May we go back to the hotel and make love before I go home?" He kissed her on the cheek and turned the boat towards the mooring.

"Over here, guv!" called the boatman. Minutes later, they were mooring with the boatman's assistance. Simon got out first, took Jennifer's hand and helped her step onto the bank. They both said thank you in unison and laughed as they walked away arm in arm and holding each other closely.

"Let's go straight back to the hotel. Your train is at two-thirty." Simon turned towards Jennifer. "We only have three hours."

CHAPTER 23

Jennifer got up from her seat by the Rayburn. She went to the fridge. I can't understand how all this has had such a dreadful effect on me. What if you had lived? She took a bottle of white wine from the fridge. What if you were still alive and we had spoken on the phone yesterday morning? She took the corkscrew from the drawer, opened the bottle and poured herself a large glass of wine. We were planning your arrival here for next week. She went through to the sitting room, but, as she was walking into the hall, the phone rang.

"Hello?"

"Jennifer, it's Carol."

"Oh, I was miles away."

"That's why I am phoning. I've made arrangements for our visit down south."

"Carol, is Peter at your house? Oh, Carol, I've been so horrid to him."

"Does he know?"

"No, but I've said the most dreadful things to him. I've hurt him. I'm so ashamed. He just went out of the back door. No goodbye, chicken, flower, lambkin - nothing. He just left the house. Do you think he might suspect something?"

"I don't know. It would be dreadful if he did."

"All these fireworks I've set loose and I would have to confess all just for one night in a hotel." The back door slammed. "He's come back, Carol. I must go." Jennifer rang off.

"I'm coming over Jennifer. Hello?" Carol said into a silent phone.

Jennifer turned to her husband. "I'm so, so sorry."

"You frightened me," said Peter. He approached her. "You and I are so different. You have always been the outgoing one, introduced me to different people. If it wasn't for you, I wouldn't have done half the things that I've achieved over the years." He took a sip of Jennifer's wine. She reached up and got another glass out of the cupboard, filling it to the top with wine.

"Here you are, my darling. I'm so sorry. I don't know what got into me."

"You are quite happy with me, aren't you?"

"Yes, I am, Peter."

He put some coal into the Rayburn and closed the door. He sat in the spare chair by the side of Jennifer. "You know that you can do anything, have anything that your heart desires?"

"I'm sorry," said Jennifer.

"As far as I'm concerned, my darling, the incident never took place." He swigged his wine. "Who was that on the phone?"

"Carol." Here goes, thought Jennifer. More lies. "She would like me to go with her down south. Her godmother has died and it's her funeral on Friday. I said I'd go with her to keep her company."

"That's fine with me. You know you don't have to ask. It will be nice for you girls to spend some time together. How kind of you to offer to accompany her." Oh, Peter, Jennifer thought, please don't go on. You make me feel even more ashamed.

"When were you thinking of leaving?"

"I don't know. Carol is going to let me know the arrangements."

"Well, today is Tuesday. Funeral on Friday. Why don't you leave tomorrow and do a bit of shopping? I can look after Bess, and Chi will understand." Chi looked up with her sad eyes at the sound of her name. "I don't have to stay in the lodge tonight."

"That's very sweet of you, but I'm fine, Peter." Lights came up the drive.

"Who's this?"

"It must be Carol," said Jennifer. "She said that she would probably come round to sort out the travel arrangements."

Sure enough, it was Carol. "Hi, Peter," she said, as she came through the door.

Peter stood up. "Hello." He kissed Carol on the cheek. "We're just having a glass of wine. Can I pour you one?

"Oh, yes please." Carol removed her coat and put it on the spare chair.

Peter handed her a glass of wine. "So sorry to hear of the death in your family."

"Oh, yes. Thank you. It's not family, Peter. An old school friend of Mummy's. She was my godmother. I thought I would go and represent Mummy because, as you know, she's too frail to go herself."

"Very kind of you, Carol, isn't it, Jennifer?"

"Yes, very kind."

He finished his wine. "I'll go and see Tom." He took some milk from the fridge. "I expect he'd like a cup of tea. I'll be back as soon as poss, lambkins." He kissed Jennifer and left but returned a few moments later and handed Jennifer the flask. "I've just found this on the doorstep."

"Oh, Margaret made me a flask of hot chocolate! I forgot to bring the flask back and Frank must have found it…" Then Jennifer remembered: "Oh, Bess!"

"She's in her stable. Frank also brought down her saddle that you'd left on the fence," said Peter.

"I'm all of a tizz!" cried Jennifer.

"I know, pet," and he went out, closing the door behind him.

Jennifer washed the flask in the sink.

"What have you done all day, Jennifer?" asked Carol. "When I left last night, I thought you were more positive. You told me you were going to tell Simon that you'd decided to stay with Peter."

"I lied," Jennifer admitted. "I was going to leave Peter. I just didn't know how you would react if I told you the truth. You said yourself, Carol, that you wouldn't have given it a second thought. Well, neither did I. I loved him to total distraction, which is now proving to be so." Tears started to spill down her cheeks. "I'm trying desperately to put my life back together, but, every moment I'm on my own, I go back to that lovely time we were together, all the things we did with each other. I didn't expect this to happen. Neither of us did. We just fell in love and now he's no longer here. I have to go on without him for the rest of my life." Jennifer poured out more wine for them both. "You see, he was coming here next week."

"What? Here?"

"No, not here - although he wanted to be with me when I told Peter, so that he could support me through my anguish. He knew how concerned I was about hurting Peter, but love hurts. Now there's nothing."

"Oh, my dearest Jennifer, I had no idea. Why didn't you tell me yesterday? Come here - let me give you a hug. Why didn't you tell me?"

"I felt ashamed of my disloyalty to Peter. Now that Simon has died, I try to put the thoughts out of my mind, but I can't help reliving them. It was so wonderful. You would have fancied him, Carol."

"What was he like?"

"He was tall, quite slim, very handsome, but what I loved most about him was his eyes. His lovely, smiling eyes. He would look at me in a certain way and I would just melt." They picked up their glasses and went through to the sitting room. Chi followed. They sat by the fire.

"Have you had anything to eat?" Carol asked.

"Nothing since breakfast."

"I'll go and make you something. How about smoked salmon on wholemeal?" Carol got up and made her way into the kitchen.

Jennifer got up and stoked up the fire, then sat back down again and patted the chair. "Come on then, Chi." Chi jumped up and curled up next to her. Jennifer was smiling when Carol returned.

"What are you smiling about?"

"I was watching the flames go up the chimney and I was thinking about the balloons that Simon bought for us when were just about to go back to our hotel to make love for the last time. It was before we had planned our next meeting." Carol handed Jennifer her sandwiches. "Thank you, Carol." Jennifer tucked in, suddenly realising how hungry she actually was. "These are very much appreciated."

"You mentioned balloons?"

"Well, we saw this sweet man selling balloons. I mentioned that I loved balloons and asked how much they were. I felt sorry for him and I said to Simon that it must be very difficult to earn a living like that and he probably had a wife and children at home. Anyway, Simon walked over and bought the lot! The man seemed very happy and left balloonless! Simon looked so sweet, coming towards me with them all. He handed me half of them, then he released his remaining balloons. They went up and up. They symbolise the past, he said. I let go of mine one at a time. The sky was full of them. They looked so pretty, floating away. People had stopped to watch and little children were trying to jump after them. We were just having so much fun. We then went back to the hotel to collect our things before we had to leave."

"Did he take you to the station?"

"Of course he did - and bought me some magazines and a drink for the journey."

Carol smiled. "I've booked us into a hotel near where the funeral will be. We can leave tomorrow or Thursday."

"Thursday will be fine, Carol."

"Judy phoned today. She said she tried to call

you, but you were out. She's invited us for lunch tomorrow and said to just come along. No need to confirm. She's looking forward to hearing your news about Lydia and the baby."

"I'd like that. It's about time I started to pull myself together and stop looking back." Jennifer got up from her seat and took her plate into the kitchen. "I'm tired with all the turmoil going on in my head."

Carol picked up her coat from the chair. "I'll pick you up at about one o'clock." She kissed Jennifer on the cheek and left. Jennifer closed the door and looked at the kitchen clock. It was nine-thirty. She filled a saucepan with milk from the fridge, took a mug from the cupboard above the dishwasher, warmed her milk, filled her mug and went towards the stairs. Chi was settling into her bed by the Rayburn. "Goodnight, my gorgeous Chi."

Jennifer went upstairs, put the warm milk on her bedside table and went into the bathroom. She started running a bath and added some lavender and bubbles under the pouring water. She returned to the bedroom, picked up her milk, went back into the bathroom and enjoyed the comforting drink before getting into the bath. The water was lovely and warm. She was surrounded by huge bubbles. Jennifer picked them up in her hands and blew them across the bath. They were perfectly round, just like those balloons.

"People must think we're totally mad, letting all those balloons go!"

"We are!" said Simon, whirling her around and around.

"Stop it! You're making me dizzy!"

"I'm here to catch you." He pulled her towards him and put his arms around her, holding her to his body. Their lips came together. "I'm so happy, Jenny, the love of my life! You and me." He let go of Jennifer and put his hand into his jacket pocket and pulled out one of the beautifully wrapped parcels. He put it into Jennifer's hand and closed her fingers over her package. "You will phone on Monday, won't you, my darling? I need to know that you will before we part today, as I've no way of getting in touch with you," Simon pleaded. Jennifer opened her bag and put the parcel inside. She slipped her bag back over her shoulder. They linked arms and started to walk.

"I promised you, didn't I? I promised Peter twenty-five years ago to honour and love."

He stopped walking briefly and turned to her. "So, you're saying that you're going to continue your contented life in Herefordshire, are you? Completely let everything die that we have between us?" He steered her towards a park seat and they sat down. "Jenny, we met and fell in love."

"I know, Simon. But surely you search your conscience about the things we've done? The hurt we've caused two people who know nothing about what we've done? I love you, Simon - my God, I do! - and I haven't felt this way ever in my life before, but will it last? Is it true love, or is it lust?"

"Lust, Jennifer? You astound me greatly," he laughed with astonishment, "I'm astounded and very hurt."

"Oh, Simon, I'm so sorry." Her eyes filled with tears. They trickled down her cheeks. "I'm so sorry. I'm scared that we might regret all the lovely things we've done."

"You're confused, aren't you, my darling?" He wiped her tears away with his warm hand.

"Yes, I am." Simon handed her his handkerchief. She blew her nose and wiped her eyes. "I feel as though I'm in a tornado, going round and round. I know my future with Peter."

"But we can have so much more," said Simon. "Just think of it! We can see the world together, play on the beach, paddle, swim. How I would love to swim with you and show things to you that I want to see myself."

Jennifer took hold of Simon's hand. "I will phone, just don't rush me. Please give me time. As far as our future is concerned, let's take time together. We'll reflect on these two wonderful days over the weekend. I think I'll be rather muddled all weekend just thinking of you."

"Oh, Jenny, of course we'll take time. I thought a moment ago you were going to forget me."

As if I could forget about you, Simon! She picked up the flowers from the dressing table, smelt them and touched them, moved the flowers that Mrs Thompson had put on the table and, in their place, she put her sweet posy close to her pillow. She slipped under the freshly laundered duvet cover and laid her head down. She turned her head so that she could see her flowers, which were emitting a hint of fragrance. She turned off the light and lay there in the moonlight, feeling cosy and warm and aroused. She touched her breasts. Her nipples were hard. She rolled them between her fingers, which then awakened other parts of her body. Her hand went down. She was very wet. Her fingers found her clitoris. You've never done this before, Jennifer told herself, as her fingers parted her fanny. She felt her clitoris and stroked it gently. She closed her eyes, increasing the rhythm of her fingers and she started to move. Oh, Simon, Simon! How can I ever forget you? She lay there, rocking her bottom gently in the bed, with her fingers still stroking her clitoris. Her fingers moved closer to her vagina and entered her body. She moved them in and out, returned her fingers to her clitoris with the moisture on her fingers and started to rub vigorously until she climaxed. The moon was still peeping through the window. The flowers smelt wonderful and she didn't cry. She fell asleep, glad that she hadn't cried.

CHAPTER 24

Jennifer awoke the next morning, having had a good night's sleep. Peter had stayed in the lodge with Tom. She became aware of voices coming from the kitchen below, so she leapt out of bed, quickly pulled on her jeans and T-shirt, then hurried into the bathroom, brushed her teeth, did her hair and put on a smattering of make-up.

"Hello, you people," said Jennifer, as she entered the kitchen.

"Did you have a good night's sleep, my darling?" asked Peter.

"Yes, thank you. I slept like a baby and feel really refreshed."

"You look much brighter," said Mrs Thompson. "You've got that glow about you back again."

"Thank you, Mrs Thompson," replied Jennifer. "I do feel better."

Mrs Thompson handed her a mug of coffee. "Would you like some toast, too?"

"No, thank you. I'm going out for lunch and I want to take Bess for a jolly good romp across the hills before I go, but thank you all the same."

"Where are you going for lunch, my pet?" asked Peter.

"Judy Ferguson's. By the way, I saw Ted when

Chi and I went to town yesterday and he offered to take Chi for a walk." Chi Chi trotted over to Jennifer and put her nose on Jennifer's knee. "Yes, we were talking about you," she said, as she tapped Chi on the nose. She went over to her riding boots, which were standing by the fire. "Ooh! These feel nice and warm," she commented, as she pulled them on. She walked towards the door and took her coat from the door hook. The ever-faithful Chi Chi was by her side. "I think you should stay here, pet," said Jennifer, as she bent down to give Chi Chi a stroke.

"She can come with me," volunteered Peter.

"I'll come and see you later – I want to see how those new lambs are doing," said Jennifer.

They walked out together. "See you in a while, Mrs Thompson!"

Peter kissed Jennifer on the cheek. "Enjoy your ride and I'll see you when you get back, darling. Come, Chi!"

Jennifer could hear the usual greetings coming from the stables. "Coming, Bess!" she called back.

"Did you enjoy that?" asked Mrs Thompson, as Jennifer walked into the kitchen after her ride.

"Yes, it was wonderful, thank you," replied Jennifer. "We had snow on the ground the last time – that was a month ago. I blew all the cobwebs from my head." Jennifer sat on the chair and pulled off her boots. Mrs Thompson put a mug of hot chocolate and a plate of biscuits on the table for her. "Oh, thank you, Mrs Thompson! I love chocolate biscuits!"

"Maggie," said Mrs Thompson. "I do prefer you to call me Maggie."

"I know you do, but 'Mrs Thompson' is more respectful and that's the way I was introduced to you. And I do respect you, Maggie. The things you do for us are greatly appreciated – like my flowers yesterday. It was a lovely surprise to go into my bedroom and see them there! The little things you do, as well…"

"You and Mr Peter – and the old departed, rest in peace – have always treated us proper, so that is my way of saying thank you. And, besides all that, I happen to like you very much and you don't treat me like a daily help – you treat me more as a friend." Mrs Thompson rinsed her coffee mug under the tap. "While you was out riding, I polished and hoovered the sitting room, tidied upstairs and hoovered the stairs. I was wondering: do you want me to prepare some vegetables for this evening?"

"Well, yes and no! I am hoping that Peter will take me out this evening. We've not had much time for each other since I've been back. On the other hand, he might not want to go out, so, yes, please!

We can always have them tomorrow."

"I'll prepare them and put them in the fridge," said Mrs Thompson.

Jennifer finished her hot chocolate. "Here's the card you asked me to buy. I hope it's what you wanted."

"Oh, that's very nice, thank you. Nice words."

"Yes, they are," agreed Jennifer. "I'm going upstairs now to have a quick bath and change. I'll see you tomorrow."

"I'll take that ironing home and do it in front of the telly tonight. Frank's got bowls and I haven't got any knitting. You know me: I like to knit! I was wondering: my Frank and me was talking the other night about me knitting a christening shawl for Noah."

"What a lovely idea! I'm sure Lydia would be thrilled. I'll buy the wool next week – tell me what you want. I must dash! I'll see you tomorrow."

With that, Jennifer hurried upstairs.

"Jennifer! Jennifer! Where are you?"

"I'm upstairs! I'm just putting the finishing touches to my face." Carol walked into the bedroom, where Jennifer was getting ready to go to lunch at Judy's. "I'm beginning to think that I'll soon be needing Polyfilla for this face."

Carol was looking at Jennifer's flowers. "I

thought Peter suffered with hay fever."

"He does. I'll remove Mrs Thompson's flowers when I get back. Yes, anyway, after a good night's sleep, I'm feeling a lot clearer in my head." Jennifer looked at her watch. You're early. I wasn't sure whether you'd be coming after our conversation."

"Of course! You look fantastic!"

"I slept really well. I took Bess for a romp this morning, which blew all the muddle from my head." Jennifer picked up her jacket.

"I wish I'd worn a skirt," commented Carol as they went downstairs into the kitchen. "Have we got time for a drink?"

"Yes, why not?" Jennifer opened the fridge. "We have wine, orange juice, tonic water, soda water …"

"I'll have a white wine spritzer – tall and long, please!"

Jennifer made two spritzers and handed one to Carol. "What would you say if I told you I've been thinking of not attending Simon's funeral?"

"You can't do that Jennifer! You must put him completely to rest in your mind. Close the book. You said that you'd like to see his family."

"That was when I was raw. It was very soon after the phone call to his office on Monday. Today is Wednesday."

"You've totally changed. You weren't like this

last night. You're the old Jennifer. What's brought about your change of mind?"

"My good night's sleep, as I've told you." She was playing with the rim of her glass. "And I masturbated."

"You what?"

"I masturbated and didn't cry. All the crying I've done over these last forty-eight hours has gone. I do feel as though things are falling back into place."

"You masturbated?"

"Yes. Why? Don't you?"

"Yes, occasionally."

"Well, then," said Jennifer. "Simon had confused my life."

"Jennifer, last night you said you loved this man."

"I do. I always will. Those forty-eight hours will never happen again and I wouldn't take the memories away for anything."

"Well, welcome back, Jennifer!" Carol put her hand onto Jennifer's hand. "I do still think we ought to go tomorrow. Charles hasn't queried anything. Have you told Peter?"

"Yes."

"Well, let's go and you can make up your mind properly when we arrive. If you decide not to go, we'll have a jolly good shop and enjoy some time together. We haven't been away together for years."

"That's true - we haven't," Jennifer agreed. "Remember that package deal to Spain and those two chaps from the stock exchange? Didn't we have fun? That was my first time." She stood up. "Time to go."

"Do you make a habit of picking up handsome chaps when you're away from home?"

"Not very often."

"Hello, my love. Did you have a good lunch and chinwag with the girls?" Peter was holding a big bouquet of flowers.

"Oh, Peter! They are lovely! Thank you!"

"Welcome home, my sweet." He kissed her tenderly on her lips and she kissed him back.

"Thank you so much. I must put them in some water immediately." She scrambled for her shoes, which she had kicked off when she returned from the lunch, and they went through to the kitchen. Jennifer took a large vase from the cupboard by the side of the sink and filled it with water. She unwrapped the flowers, which were beautifully arranged by the florist, and placed them carefully in the vase.

"Would you like to go out this evening?" Peter asked.

"Darling, that would be lovely! I can wear the new dress I bought just before I went away."

"Oh, well, in that case, I'll give Juliano's a ring and book a table," and he went through to the hall. Jennifer looked at her flowers. What a lovely surprise! Peter does do surprising things sometimes and he knew that flowers would cheer me up. I'm so lucky.

Peter returned. "All done. We've got a table at eight-thirty."

"I'm looking forward to that," smiled Jennifer.

"I thought that it should be a little special, in view of airing your new frock."

"Dress, Peter! You are so old-fashioned!" she said, as she picked up the vase of flowers and carried it through to the sitting room.

"Oh, sorry, my pet."

Jennifer returned. "I love you for it, silly! It makes you unique. Thank you for my flowers," and she kissed him on the cheek.

"You look lovely," said Peter admiringly, as Jennifer entered the sitting room later, wearing her new dress.

"Thank you! I feel good. Do you like my flowers?" Jennifer glanced at the lovely flowers, which were now bringing life to the sitting room.

"I always like the way you have with flowers. The room has been dead without flowers for three weeks," he said, handing her a glass of champagne.

"It's all right. I've ordered a taxi for eight and I did a bit of shopping while I was out this afternoon." He put his hand in his jacket pocket. "This is for you, my darling." It was a beautifully tied little parcel.

"For me?"

"Yes. I missed you so much."

"Can I open it now?"

"Yes, my darling."

She took it from him. He held her glass for her while she opened the little parcel. Inside was a box containing an eternity ring. "Oh, Peter! I've always wanted one. You remembered!"

"Let me put it on your finger." He put her glass down on the table next to his. She removed her engagement ring and put it on the mantelpiece.

"It fits! It's lovely! Oh, thank you, thank you!" She threw her arms around his neck. "I've always, always wanted one."

"I know," replied Peter. She was holding her hand up, so that the diamonds all around the ring could catch the light.

"Do you remember when Carol got hers?"

"Yes, I do," Peter confirmed. "The little green-eyed monster!"

"Just a little! How did you know my size?"

"Your jewellery box. I nipped in this morning while you were riding Bess - I was glad you removed the flowers, by the way." He handed Jennifer back her glass. "Me and my hay fever..." Jennifer had taken the little posy and returned it to her dressing table. She would probably throw them away tomorrow. Peter sat on the sofa. "Come and sit here." He patted the seat and Jennifer sat next to him. He put his hand on her knee. "You know, my darling, I don't know what I would do if I ever lost you. You are my life. When you were in Kuwait, I even began to have silly thoughts. What if you met somebody over there: a handsome doctor, maybe, while Lydia and Michael are taking you out socialising? You're a very beautiful lady and I'm not sophisticated like you. I'm just a humble farmer."

"Peter, you silly goat! You have always been my rock. I depend on you."

"But do you love me?" he asked. She moved closer to him.

"Yes, Peter. I love you very much." She held her hand out in front of her again, just to admire the sparkling ring.

Peter refilled her glass. "I clearly need to think of something else for our wedding anniversary!" he laughed.

CHAPTER 25

"Mr and Mrs Darling, would you like to come this way?" The waiter showed them to their table. Peter waited until Jennifer had sat down, then he took her shawl and bag from her and put them on the spare chair by his side. He touched her hand tenderly and squeezed her fingers.

"You look lovely."

"Thank you, Peter. You always know the right thing to say."

"I know you. We've been together a long time."

She smiled. "And you, too, look very handsome in your suit." She straightened his tie. The waiter came to their table.

"What would you like, my darling?" asked Peter.

"Calamari to start, please. And for the main … It says here: lobster when available."

"It is available today, madam."

"Then I shall have lobster with salad, please."

"And I'll have chef's soup to start, please, followed by steak au poivre with vegetables," said Peter.

The waiter smiled in acknowledgement. "Would you like to order wine?"

"I think we'll stick to champagne, please. Bring the best of the house." Peter turned to Jennifer.

"After all, we're also celebrating the birth of our grandson! Grandma and Grandpa!"

"Oh, don't Peter. It makes me feel so old."

"But you're not, my pet."

"I just hate the thought of Noah calling me Grandma. I love him, but the thought of that grates on me."

"We'll have to think of another handle for you, won't we?"

"It's a little way ahead before he starts to talk. I don't suppose we'll see them very much, now that they're a family," said Jennifer, sadly. "It's difficult travelling with babies and it's an extremely long flight."

"Yes, it is. How did you cope on such a long journey?"

"Just fine. The stewardesses were very helpful." She smiled. "I had supper, watched a film – well, glanced, really."

"Oh, what film was it?"

"I forget. It sounded very violent."

Juliano was approaching their table. Saved by the champagne, thought Jennifer, breathing a sigh of relief.

"Your champagne, Mr Darling."

"Good evening, Juliano."

"Good evening, Mrs Darling. Nice to see you both." He put the bucket by Peter's side and opened the bottle expertly. "Are you celebrating something special?"

"Just having my wife home." Peter tapped Jennifer's hand.

"Oh, where have you been?" Juliano asked, as he filled the champagne flutes.

"Kuwait."

"Ah, the bambino! It has arrived?"

"Yes, a month ago."

Juliano handed Jennifer her glass. "The last time you were here was Christmas and you mentioned that Lydia was pregnant. Now you are Grandma and Grandpa!"

"See, look! Doesn't it sound old?" cried Jennifer.

"No," retorted Peter, "I think it sounds quite comfortable. Think of it this way, my darling. What if Lydia had married Ted? We would probably have a herd of grandchildren by now and they would be calling you Grandma every day. Ted would have had Lydia pregnant all the time. You've escaped that!"

"I have, haven't I? Gosh, what a thought!"

Peter laughed. "It won't be so bad being called Grandma occasionally then?"

"No, I suppose not," she laughed.

They continued their lighthearted chat as they ate their starters. Once they had finished, the waiter returned to clear their plates.

"That was lovely, thank you, Peter. I really enjoyed it," said Jennifer. Another waiter appeared with their main courses. "As it happens," Jennifer continued, "I saw Ted yesterday afternoon when I nipped into town."

"Yes, he told me he had seen you earlier. He still holds a torch for Lids."

"It's 'carries a candle', you silly sausage."

"Well, they both light up, don't they?"

"Yes, my sweet." They both laughed.

"He talks about her a lot," said Peter. "He's a nice lad. It would have been quite beneficial to both firms had they married. They could have had the farmhouse."

"No, Peter. I would never give up my house. I love my home."

"Well, we could have had a house built on the land for them, then. He could've taken over all my duties until Judy and Cliff retire, then we would've been able to travel and see the world."

"You've never said that before, Peter. I thought you didn't like travelling."

"It's not that I haven't wanted to - more that we've never had the time. I did a lot of thinking while you were away, Jennifer - soul searching. I know you're reasonably happy. I am extremely happy," Jennifer went to stop him. "Please, let me finish. Three weeks is a long time without you: an idle house, lots of long lonely nights, lying in bed, realising how much I neglect you. I want to start spending more time with you. We have less time in front of us than we do behind us. Time is short, so, while you were away, I contemplated selling the farm."

"Oh, no, Peter! It's your life." She touched his arm.

"Alternatively, we could get in a working couple to take over, completely manage the farm."

"Oh, Peter! Where would we live?"

"Anywhere – or, if you're determined to keep the farmhouse, we'll build a house on the land for them."

The waiter returned and removed their empty main course plates.

"My lobster was absolutely delicious, thank you."

"And my steak was perfect. Do send our compliments to the chef." Peter smiled at Jennifer. "Coffee, darling?"

"No, thank you."

"Just our bill then, please."

Juliano approached their table. He was holding a tray bearing two drinks.

"This is for you, Mrs Darling: your favourite – Cointreau frappé - and a brandy for you, Mr Darling."

"Thank you! Welcome home." Peter raised his glass to Jennifer.

"Isn't that kind?" remarked Jennifer, approving of drinks on the house. The candles were reflecting in the ice in her drink, and the diamonds in her eternity ring were flickering. "Look how it shines, Peter!"

"You're a funny button; always amusing. Where's your other ring?"

"It's on the mantelpiece at home. I just wanted to wear this one on its own for this evening."

"You are a funny little goose. That's why I love you so much."

"I did enjoy that," smiled Jennifer. "Thank you for a lovely evening."

"It was very kind of Juliano to add the finishing touches."

Juliano approached their table. "Your taxi is here, Mr Darling."

"Thank you, Juliano."

"Always lovely to see you both."

Peter handed Jennifer her bag and draped her shawl around her shoulders. "See you soon, Juliano. Thank you. Goodbye… Oh! My bill! I'm so sorry!"

"I'll send it to you in the post, Mr Darling."

"Thank you very much, goodnight."

Once home, Jennifer removed her shawl and put down her bag. "I feel quite tired with all the excitement of this evening and the champagne," she said, as they both walked into the sitting room. Jennifer went over to the mantelpiece, picked up her engagement ring and placed it carefully into the little eternity ring box. "If you want to go to the barn, I quite understand."

"You don't mind?" He came over to her and put his arms around her and kissed her. It was just like the old Peter, whom she met and fell in love with all those years ago.

"You certainly have changed," she said.

"There's always room for improvement! I'll quickly change and then go over to the barn. I hope we can continue the conversation that we had this evening. I do want us to have a better future, Jennifer."

"Yes, I know. I think your idea about the couple is something we must talk about at length this weekend."

Peter smiled. "Okey dokey, my chicken. See you later."

Jennifer was in bed reading her book when Peter came back.

"I thought you'd be asleep."

"No, I was waiting for you."

"Well, my petal," he said, as he sat on the bed. "It's not going too well for one of the ewes. It's her first year. Frank isn't at home."

"I know," agreed Jennifer. "He has a bowls' night away match, I think."

"I can't let Billy cope on his own. He doesn't have the experience."

"Are you trying to say, Peter, that you think that you ought to go back?"

"Yes."

"Go! As you said, lambing season doesn't last forever. I'll probably go to sleep now, anyway." He leant towards her, kissed her on the lips and left the room. Jennifer put down her book and turned out the light. Things were so different now, she thought. Did all those things happen with Simon? It was all becoming quite fuzzy in her mind. The moon was shining through the window and she put her hand into the beam. Her diamonds shone brightly. What a lovely surprise! How could I ever have contemplated leaving Peter? I must have been mad even thinking about doing it. Simon completely swept me off my feet. It can't possibly have been love. And now I'm home with my wonderful, darling husband. Her eyes started to flicker sleepily and they closed.

"Champagne - yes! I ordered it when I paid the bill this morning. I thought it was quite a fitting send-off for us both, as we go on our separate journeys - until the next time we see each other." Jennifer took off her coat, Simon removed his jacket and they sat down on the sofa. Simon opened the champagne with a loud pop. "Quick! Grab the glasses!" Jennifer held both glasses under the over-exuberant flow.

"I think we caught most of it!" Jennifer handed him his glass. "What should we drink to?" she asked.

"Our future: Darby and Joan."

"You Darby, me Joan." They both laughed.

"To the future." They clinked their glasses and drank it down quickly.

"Wow!" marvelled Jennifer. "I've only ever sipped champagne. It makes me feel quite woozy."

"More wooziness?" Simon refilled her glass and placed his glass on the table. He pulled up the chair and sat opposite Jennifer. He leant forward and kissed her lips. "I'm going to miss these lips."

"We've had a lovely time, haven't we?"

"Yes, we have." He took hold of her hands. "To think, if I hadn't seen you at the airport, none of this would have happened."

"No, we have Lydia to thank for that," said Jennifer. "She's the one that spotted you."

"So, Lydia caused all this to happen? She's responsible for you and me?"

"Yes. She'll giggle when I tell her that we spent

the journey home together."

"Will you tell Peter?"

"No - although I think, if I did, he would say well done - much better to have company rather than being on my own. He would hope that we'd both enjoyed each other's company. I don't think it would have bothered him."

"Will you tell him all?"

"Don't be silly, Simon! Tell him about the plane - and this?" Jennifer said, pointing towards the bed.

Simon laughed. "I like to see you flustered."

"You do, don't you? You beast!" He put Jennifer's glass down next to his and stood her up. He unbuttoned her shirt.

"Time to kiss you better," he said. Her shirt slid off her shoulders. She removed it and put it on the chair. He removed her skirt and put it neatly on top of her shirt, then he removed his clothes very quickly and put them on the bedside chair. It amused her. He knelt on the floor and started to undo her suspenders. Her stockings fell to the floor and she wriggled her toes free of them, dropping her suspender belt to the floor on top of them. Simon picked them up, stood up and walked over to the chair, neatly putting them where her other clothes were. "Are you wearing these clothes to go back home in?" he asked.

"No, I'm wearing my comfy trousers."

"Ah, in that case…" and he picked them up and threw them onto his pile.

"You are funny!" giggled Jennifer.

Simon again knelt on the floor. His hands came up towards the top of her panties. He slipped them down her legs and Jennifer kicked them out of the way. Simon kissed her inner thigh and gradually moved up her body. Just the thought of his lips going where she knew they were aiming for made her excited. He stood up in front of her and removed her bra. There they were, standing to attention, neither knowing which would be first. He put his arms around her waist and that feeling she had become familiar with over the past couple of days came over her. His hands then drifted gently around to her breasts, which he cupped and rolled under his palm. He opened his fingers so that her nipples could poke through. Closing his fingers, he clamped her nipples and moved his hands up and down. The feeling was sensational! He kissed her. His body was so close to hers - any closer and he would be behind her. She could feel his masculinity poking her tummy. His arms went around her waist as he moved her towards the bed and continued kissing her.

"What about the sheets?"

"When I paid the bill this morning, I paid for an extra day."

He pulled back the duvet and sat her on the bed with her feet on the floor. He opened her legs, pressing little kisses all the way up her thigh. His lips kissed her ever-moist mound, his tongue finding her little bud. The tip of his tongue circled around, then pulled it into his warm mouth. Here we go again! thought Jennifer, as she responded by moving her body to the rhythm of his mouth. She eased herself onto the bed and Simon joined her. He lay next to her and she slid on top of him, moved down his body and rested her head on his chest. She kissed his nipples. "I like that," he moaned. She sucked them and rubbed her hand on his lovely curly chest. She moved down towards the ultimate goal. Her lips kissed it to the side and the top. Then she opened her mouth and let it slip inside. She moved her mouth up and down. Simon was groaning beautifully. Her hand was holding his scrotum and moving it around. "Oh Jenny, Jenny I love you." She kissed his thigh. Simon lifted his head from the pillow and pulled her close to him. They kissed. He lay her down and moved his body down hers.

"No, Simon, I just want to make love."

"We will." He kissed her again and moved further down her body, a body he had become very familiar with. His mouth was quenched by her moisture, his lips sucking her bud.

"Oh, Simon, Simon!" She climaxed. Simon moved with even more confidence. He pulled her bottom towards his and grasped her buttocks, pushing himself deeply into her vagina. She wrapped her legs around him, squeezing them together. He held her tightly and rolled her over. They were still attached. She was now on top and was moving up and down as he moved in and out. Jennifer leant down and kissed him. She put her hands on his chest, so that she could roll her bottom on his groin. Her bud was brushing his groin and she could feel that wonderful sensation rising up her body. His hands cupped her breasts and rolled her nipples.

"I'm going wild," Jennifer groaned.

"I know. I love it when you go wild."

She knelt over his body. He held her bottom down on his groin as they climaxed together. She lay on his chest, his fingers gently stroking her shoulder. "Aren't we perfect together?"

"Yes, we are," smiled Jennifer. As his breathing gradually slowed down, she rolled off and lay by his side.

"We've been together since ten-fifteen on Wednesday night in Kuwait," said Simon, "and so much has happened. We've packed a lot into the little time we've had together."

"Yes, I feel quite exhausted," agreed Jennifer,

smiling contentedly.

"I hope you're happily exhausted." He put his arm around her shoulder.

"Oh, yes, of course. I wouldn't have wanted it any other way. I just wish we had more time together and hadn't had to fit so much into such a short time."

"What a pity we didn't meet in Kuwait," said Simon.

"Yes, that would have been lovely."

"Where were you staying?"

"Lydia and Michael live near the hospital. They have a very nice villa - not that huge, but it's in a complex of large houses by the hospital."

"I stayed in a hotel just down the road from there, on the sea front!" Simon said excitedly. "I must have passed where you were every day en route to my appointments! We were meant to meet. Fate didn't achieve its intention to have us meet there, so it made sure we would meet at the airport."

They were starting to get dressed.

"Do you believe in fate?" asked Jennifer.

"Oh, yes! We met, didn't we? I don't usually pick up beautiful ladies at airports. It's funny," he said. "I suppose, deep down, when I saw you in the departure lounge, I knew that we were going to become connected somehow. No lady has ever taken my eye the way you did. I fancied you as soon as I saw you. I waited for you to find your seat on the plane first and then I pounced." He pounced playfully towards her.

"Really? Had you already planned to ask me to spend the night with you?"

"I just knew that I needed to talk to you. I liked you." He was putting on his tie now.

"I love you in a suit. That's how I first saw you," said Jennifer, straightening his tie. She kissed him on his chin.

"There's a drop of champers left. Should I divide it equally?"

"Yes, please," They sat on the bed. "When did you start thinking about suggesting suggestions towards me?"

"Ah, well, that came later."

"With the gin and tonic?"

"No, no," he smiled.

"You are one big tease, Simon Lawson!" Jennifer went to her bag. "Where's your little plane?"

"In my suitcase, inside my sports jacket pocket." He came over to her and put his arms around her waist. "Do you really want to know when I thought about suggesting suggestions to you?"

"Yes."

"When you walked up that staircase in front of me on the plane. It's these legs. I'm a serial legs man. Your face isn't bad either."

"Go away, you beast!"

"Oh, Jenny, I love all of you - especially your legs - and now you have these ridiculous trousers on!"

"I don't think I'll be able to wear trousers again in your company."

"You most certainly won't!" agreed Simon.

"I like trousers. They're comfortable."

"Well, perhaps I'll allow you to wear them occasionally. Now, we have to put all this frivolity to one side, my darling Jenny. Time is seriously marching on." Simon was looking at the luggage. "I think we need a porter and a taxi."

"The fishing rod! Oh, Simon! I forgot about the fishing rod! It will be at reception." Jennifer gathered her things. "Bye room! Thank you."

Simon closed the door as they left. "You really amuse me!" he smiled. "Come on! You have a train to catch." They went down to the reception desk and enquired about the fishing rod.

"Yes, we have the rod. It was delivered by Harrods this morning."

"I'll find us a porter and a taxi." Simon said, heading off on his mission.

"Madam, here it is. Will you please sign for it?" asked the receptionist.

"Yes, of course." She signed Mrs Green, The

Meadows, Ickley, Herefordshire.

"We make a note of your address and send you some of the hotel theatre offers that we have during the year and also our Christmas offers."

"Thank you very much."

Jennifer took the rod back to her luggage, where Simon was waiting. "They gift-wrapped it. Weren't they kind?"

"How are you going to disguise it? Could we unscrew it?" suggested Simon.

"Yes, I'll do it on the train."

CHAPTER 26

The taxi arrived and the luggage was packed into the boot. Jennifer got into the cab, followed by Simon, who sat next to her. "Paddington Station, please," he said to the taxi driver.

"My eyes are beginning to feel all watery," said Jennifer.

He put both his hands on her hands. "It won't be long. We'll talk on Monday and through the week until I come down the following week."

Once at the station, they made their way to the platform together. "Here's your train - dead on two-thirty."

A station porter assisted them with the suitcases and they followed the luggage onto the train. "Here's a nice seat by the window, next to the refreshments carriage." Simon put down the magazines that he had bought for Jennifer on their way into the station. She stood by her seat, not wanting to sit down yet. "I don't want you to go," he said.

"I don't want to either, but I must go home and put my thoughts together." Further down the train, the heavy doors started to slam, one by one. "I can't wait to hear your voice on Monday morning. Listen to me! I'm beginning to miss you already and we haven't even parted yet."

"Oh, Jenny!" He held her close. "My darling Jennifer Darling."

"Go, go! You're making it more difficult." He kissed her and held her tighter, knowing they only had seconds left together. "Go, please, Simon." His hands slipped away and he stepped out onto the platform. She pulled the door shut and opened the window. There were people moving about quickly all around him.

He reached up, held her hand and kissed it. "Speak to you on Monday, my darling." The train started to leave the station. He moved quickly along the platform with the train.

"Bye! Love you!" Jennifer called, as she blew him a kiss and waved. Then he was gone.

Peter crept into the bedroom. He had undressed in the bathroom so as not to disturb Jennifer. He slid in beside her and put his arms around her waist. He moved her body closer to his, though he knew she was asleep, as she was snoring sweetly. He hugged her and went to sleep by the side of his beloved. Jennifer stirred and wiggled her body closer.

Jennifer was in the kitchen when Peter came in through the door. "I could smell the bacon as I came up the yard." He gave Jennifer a kiss. "Good morning, lambkins."

"I thought we could have a nice breakfast."

Peter sat down at the table. "Oh, lovely! Grilled bacon, wholemeal toast and scrambled eggs. Aren't I lucky?" Jennifer poured his tea and handed his cup to him. "I see your ring is still glistening."

"I know! Isn't it lovely? I love it. Thank you, thank you, my darling." She threw her arms around his neck.

"Steady on! You'll strangle me!"

"I'm sorry. I'm just so happy. Sit down and have your breakfast." She sat opposite him. "Was that ewe okay last night?"

"Yes. She gave birth soon after I returned. You were asleep when I came back. I slipped in by the side of you and cuddled you."

"I know - you woke me."

"I'm sorry."

"It's fine. I fell right back to sleep immediately afterwards."

"It's good to have breakfast together again."

"Yes, it is. We had a lovely evening, didn't we?"

"Yes, it was a very special evening and good for me - particularly to get those things off my chest." Mrs Thompson walked into the kitchen. "Good morning, Mrs Thompson."

"Good morning, Mr Peter and Mrs Darling.

What time will you be leaving today, Mrs Darling?"

"Oh, yes, I'd completely forgotten! Sometime this afternoon."

Peter rose from the table. "Thank you, my sweet. That was a lovely breakfast." He carried his plate, cup and saucer to the draining board. "I'll be back for elevenses." He kissed Jennifer and went off.

Jennifer was looking at her ring. "Look, Mrs Thompson! Isn't it lovely?" She held her hand up to show Mrs Thompson. "Mr Peter gave it to me just before we went out to dinner last night."

"It's very nice, Mrs Darling. You're a lucky lady."

"I'm going to ride Bess," said Jennifer with a smile. "I'll be back at eleven." She made her way outside and was suddenly troubled by the brief conversation she had just had with Mrs Thompson. Perhaps I was a little insensitive, showing my ring to Maggie. She has never had the privileges that I've had. I'm sure that she would like to have owned a lovely ring. Tears filled her eyes. Mrs Thompson was right. She really was a lucky lady.

Jennifer took Bess for a long ride, accompanied by Chi. They went on their usual route and, afterwards, Jennifer left Bess in the top field for a graze. Feeling better for the fresh air, she headed back to the farmhouse.

"Mrs Tyler phoned. She'll ring back about

eleven-thirty."

"Thank you, Mrs Thompson."

"I polished the dining room. I thought you might be having a dinner party this weekend."

"Funnily enough," said Jennifer, "I thought about that whilst I was out riding." She sat by the Rayburn and pulled off her boots. "I think Chi is a bit tired. She did well, trying to keep up with Bess and me." Chi was already curled up in her basket.

Peter came through the door. Mrs Thompson put two mugs in front of them and a plate of biscuits. "Years ago, when I was very small, in this very kitchen," said Peter, "elevenses meant mid-morning breakfast. We even had sweetbreads on toast, or cream crackers and sandwich spread - all homemade. There was none of that manufactured stuff you can buy nowadays. When we had harvests, this kitchen used to be full of men from the surrounding farms, who came to help us."

"It's a long time since you spoke about this, Peter."

"Yes, I know. Quite strange. We were talking about it at market the other day. How things have changed. There were no subsidies in those days. We all helped each other. At harvest time, tractors from the whole area would line the fields and shine their lights into the field, so that the harvest could be collected and stored whilst the weather was good.

My mother worked day and night until the task was done. Then, they would all move on to the next farm and do it all over again. It's all changed now, though."

"I remember that, Mr Peter. That was when my Frank and me got married all them years ago. He couldn't afford a wedding ring, so we used a brass curtain ring. It was on my finger for years. This one's gold." She extended her weathered hand out towards Jennifer, who looked up to admire the ring. The phone rang.

"I'll go," said Jennifer. "It's probably Carol." Saved by the bell, she thought as she picked up the phone.

"I spoke to Mrs Thompson earlier. Where were you?" asked Carol.

"Out with Bess and Chi. What time are you coming over?"

"I can come now," said Carol.

"Okay. See you in a mo." Jennifer returned to the kitchen. "Carol is on her way now. I wish I hadn't said that I would go with her. I don't want to leave you."

"You must. You did say that you would."

Carol was at the door a few minutes later and Peter welcomed her. "Hello, Carol. You're the one taking my lovely wife away from me again! Only teasing!" he laughed. "Look after her. She's very precious to me." Peter then kissed Jennifer. "I'll see you before you go," he said and went out into the yard.

"Come in, Carol," said Jennifer. The two of them sat down at the kitchen table. "Look what Peter gave me yesterday evening before we went to Juliano's."

"It's lovely Jennifer! Do the diamonds go all the way round?"

"Yes. Look! Do you remember when you got your eternity ring and how I said that I would like one as well?"

"Yes, I do," replied Carol, "but mine doesn't have diamonds going all the way round, though. It's so pretty. I hope that you gave Peter an extra big kiss."

"I certainly did," said Jennifer.

"So, you were at Juliano's last night when I rang?"

"Yes. It was quite an evening in many ways. Peter, while I was away, had been contemplating selling the farm, apparently."

"What!"

"Indeed," confirmed Jennifer. "He was thinking of selling the farm, so that he and I could spend more time together - travel the world."

"He's never spoken about this before!" said Carol, surprised. "It must be the male menopause!"

They both laughed.

"He said, while I was in Kuwait, he'd spent lonely nights in an empty bed. He said that three weeks is a long time alone in a house and it makes you reflect on an awful lot of things."

"Sounds very serious," commented Carol.

"In all, it was a lovely evening. It made me wonder if we should really go today. There's no reason for me to go. I only knew him for a very short time. Oh! I feel so confused."

Worrying that their conversation might be overheard, Carol hastily closed the kitchen door to the hall. "Jennifer, I've made the arrangements. Let's go."

"I feel so dreadful, dragging you into my deception, but I'm not sure I need to go. It must be awful for his family, but what good would I do by attending his funeral?"

"It would put it all behind you. You could start a new chapter with Peter when we come back tomorrow."

"Yes, I've not known where my mind is. I've spent every spare moment thinking about Simon, reliving everything we did… Yes, let's go."

"Thank goodness for that," breathed Carol, greatly relieved. "I don't know about you, but I'll be glad when tomorrow is over, so we can both come down to earth. You've worried me so much this week, Jennifer."

"I think Peter has been worried, too. I think he thought he'd lost me, that I'd met a doctor whilst I was staying with Liddy."

"What! He said that?"

"Yes. He looked so sad. If Simon had lived and I had decided to leave Peter, what then? I dread to think, Carol."

"It won't happen," Carol reassured her.

"No, thank God," said Jennifer. She picked up their mugs and put them in the dishwasher. "I'll go upstairs and put a few overnight things in a case."

"You'll feel better tomorrow - I know you will."

"Thank you for being a true friend."

Carol accompanied her friend upstairs and they decided together which clothes Jennifer should pack for their brief trip. Forty-five minutes and many indecisions later, the packing was complete and the two friends set off in Carol's car.

"Here are the directions. Charles worked the route out for us," said Carol.

"I'm looking forward to spending some proper time with you."

"You can tell me all about Jonathan in Spain," suggested Carol.

"That's far too long ago! An awful lot of water has gone under the bridge since then!"

"How old were we?"

"Seventeen," replied Jennifer.

"Gosh, were we really that young?"

"Yes - and that promiscuous!" replied Jennifer, laughing.

"Speak for yourself! Which way now?"

"Left at the next roundabout. Oh dear, Carol! We're getting closer. That signpost said Eastbourne."

"Good afternoon."

"Hello," said Carol. "We have two single rooms booked in my name, Carol Tyler. The other is for my friend, Jennifer Darling."

"Yes, your rooms are ready. Would you please sign in? Dinner is from seven-thirty onwards. You can either eat in the dining room, or in the bar."

They went upstairs to the bedrooms and arrived at Jennifer's room first. "I think I'll go and have a lie down," she said. "I'll see you in the bar at about seven."

"Okay." Carol kissed her on her cheek and went to find her own room.

Jennifer entered her room and walked over to the window. She gazed in the direction that she thought might be where he had lived. Here I am, Simon. Totally different from how we were going to meet. She was now pleased that she had come and very grateful that Carol had brought her here. She popped her head through the door of the bathroom. Thank goodness for an ensuite, she thought. There was a kettle and a teapot and the usual coffee, tea bags and that horrid milk that you seem to get in all hotels. She made herself a cup of tea, moved the chair, so that she could look through the window, and sat down. It was a lovely view: very rural, similar to home, with lambs scampering about. It was so sweet of Peter to come running towards them when they were about to leave, carrying a lovely little baby lamb under his arm. "She had twins and rejected this one just for you to look after, so you have to come back to look after her."

"I'll be back tomorrow!" Bess neighed as she was leaving and Chi looked up at her. I'll never leave any of you ever again. No more adventures without Peter. We'll do them together.

CHAPTER 27

Carol was already sitting in the bar. "How long have you been sitting here?" asked Jennifer.

"Half an hour."

"I fell asleep."

"I thought you probably would." Carol handed Jennifer a glass of wine.

"It's a lovely fire. Should we eat in here?" asked Jennifer, looking around the cosy room.

"Yes – good idea! Here's the menu. I've already chosen what I'm having."

Jennifer took the menu from Carol. "Thank you. Let's enjoy this evening," she said, raising her glass.

"Yes, let's," replied Carol.

"What have you chosen?"

"The lamb chops and all the trimmings. There are some chef's specials over there." Carol pointed to a board.

"I'll have trout and salad. I don't want lamb. This is the only time of the year I refuse to eat lamb. I can't eat it while they're all scampering about in the fields of England."

"You are funny, Jennifer! I'll go and order our food."

Jennifer looked around the room, noticing how much cosier it was than her local. They obviously cater for couples rather than just farmers, she thought. Carol came back to their table. "I was just thinking how pretty this bar is. The lifestyle must be totally different from where we come from," Jennifer observed.

"They commute to London from here," commented Carol.

"Yes, of course they do. Simon does…did. It's quite eerie being so close to him but knowing that he's lying somewhere in his coffin. This time last week, he was so very much alive. We were having a lovely bath together - about to go out for the evening…"

Their food arrived, along with another bottle of wine, which Carol poured for both of them. "What was he like, this man that shared your bath? A thoroughly nice chap, as Peter would say?"

"He was funny. Made me laugh all the time. Amusing and an enormous tease. I would not change the time that we spent together for anything. We meant a great deal to each other. It was as if we had known each other all our lives." Carol poured more wine. "Cheers," Jennifer said. "We haven't clinked our glasses."

"Cheers, Jennifer."

The waitress brought their food. "Gosh! That looks good!" said Carol. "I'm ready for this."

"Yes, me, too," agreed Jennifer. "Now, where

was I? Oh, yes. It's funny really. We were so natural with each other. We were perfect strangers, who met and fell in love. We were attracted to each other at the airport. He swept past and turned my head. He did - no one else. I met colleagues of Michael's in Kuwait - handsome doctors – and I didn't give them a second thought. I've known Peter for twenty-eight years and been married to him for twenty-five of those. I can honestly say, in all that time, nobody else has interested me. Peter was - and is - the love of my life, until that dratted man upset the applecart and, now, we're here to literally bury him," said Jennifer, miserably.

"Did he have family besides his wife?"

"Yes. Two sons. One of them is a doctor, the other is a solicitor, like him, and he's in the same practice in London, along with Simon's brother."

"All three solicitors?" asked Carol.

"Yes."

"In the same practice?"

"Yes, why?"

"Oh, nothing. Just a thought." Carol took a sip of her wine.

"A thought? What do you mean?"

"Jennifer, when you phoned on Monday, did they say which Mr Lawson had died?"

"Yes."

"Are you sure?"

"No. Yes... I don't know. If he'd still been alive, don't you think he would have tried to get in touch with me, knowing that I had said that I was going to ring on Monday morning? Oh, Carol, stop it! It was Simon... I'm sure his secretary said that it was Simon. Anyway, this time tomorrow, it will all be over and then we can go home." Jennifer paused to take another sip of her wine. "I was thinking about having a dinner party on Saturday evening. If it's nice weather, Peter can use his culinary skills with the barbecue - he enjoys that. I'll invite Judy and Clifford – and you and Charles, of course. We can celebrate Peter's birthday and I'll give him the fishing rod, which I know he'll love."

"That sounds very nice," replied Carol. "With all this baby business and you being away, our social life has been on hold!"

"It has rather, hasn't it. I was so worried about Liddy."

"It's heartbreaking, her being so far away. Is there any chance of them coming back to the UK?" asked Carol.

"I'll work on that when they come back for the christening. I need her home, Carol. Anywhere in this country. Michael is an exceptional gynaecologist. He can get a job anywhere in England."

"You scheming madam!" laughed Carol.

"I know! I just want us to be a family again."

Having finished their meal, they got up from the table, collected their room keys from reception and went up to their rooms. "Goodnight, Carol, and thank you for this evening." They hugged each other, two friends providing the special support that friends do.

"Good morning. Did you sleep okay?"

"Yes, thank you," replied Jennifer. "Did you?"

"Yes, like a top!" Carol was reading the local newspaper and had come across the article about the local solicitor being fatally injured. "I've already had breakfast. I had it in my room."

"So did I," said Jennifer. "I hate having to go into hotel dining rooms at breakfast time. Everyone always looks half asleep anyway. Horrible."

"I've ordered a pot of coffee," said Carol.

"Oh, thank you. What are you reading?" enquired Jennifer.

"The local rag," said Carol, as she put the paper down. "What time are you leaving?"

"I thought about ten. It's only two and a half miles down the road - I noticed the signpost as we came into the village yesterday afternoon. I'll go to reception and order a taxi."

"I'll take you."

"No, Carol, I prefer to go on my own. I'll be less

conspicuous. So, what's in the local paper?" Carol showed her the headlines: 'Solicitor from local family killed in car crash on B345. For information regarding funeral arrangements, turn to page 5'. Carol started to open the paper.

"Don't Carol, please don't! Seeing it on the front page is enough. I feel quite faint.

Please turn the paper over." Her eyes welled up.

The waitress brought their coffee and Jennifer gave her five pounds. "Keep the change," she smiled.

After the waitress had left them, Carol laughed, incredulous "Five pounds for a pot of coffee? It's not Ritz prices here, you know! I doubt a pot of coffee is even that much there."

"We didn't have coffee or tea there."

"What did you drink?" asked Carol, intrigued.

"Champagne! It's all a blur now, but, this time last week, we had just left our hotel on our final morning together." She picked up her cup of coffee. "We walked into the park, arm in arm, and found ourselves a nice place to have our breakfast. I saw a lovely older lady and gentleman. They passed quite close to us and the lady smiled. They looked so happy. Simon compared them to us in years to come. Daft things! Two people, who have just met and fallen in love, rowing on the lake." She took a sip of coffee. "I swear, if there had been a canopy, he would have made love to me on the boat."

"What, right there?"

"Yes," said Jennifer. "He was like an animal - and I loved it. I've never been overenthusiastic with Peter about things that go on in our bed, but, with Simon, we were wild. We just could not get enough of each other. It was wonderful!" Jennifer paused suddenly and looked away. "I don't think I'll go to the funeral. There's no reason why I should."

"Well, if you feel like that and you have really made up your mind not to go... Though you have come this far, Jennifer. Perhaps just go and pay your last respects. I'll be waiting here for you."

"Yes, yes... I suppose you're right... I'll go and order that taxi." Jennifer left her friend in front of the fire. Carol picked up the local paper again and turned to page five, but she heard Jennifer returning and quickly put the paper down.

"What are you going to do whilst I am away?" asked Jennifer.

"I noticed a garden centre as we were driving into the village yesterday."

"Oh, yes. I saw that, too. Mr Pike, our gardener, has been tidying up the garden for summer and there are a few plants that I would like to buy. Can we go when I come back?"

"I'll go first," said Carol, "and then we can go together on our way home. We could do some shopping in Croydon, too, perhaps."

"Yes, let's do that," agreed Jennifer. "I just want this over now. What's the time?"

"It's nine-forty-five; you booked the taxi for ten."

"Yes, that's right. I couldn't remember. Oh, Carol, I'm so glad you're here."

"I hope there won't be any questions when we get home."

"No, I don't think there will be. I do want to phone Peter, but I'm too nervous. Just attending this funeral and the thought of having betrayed him. What got into me? Some monster deep down inside me. I wasn't unhappy, so why did I sleep with another man?"

"For the excitement?" suggested Carol.

"No, it wasn't that."

"If Simon had still been alive, would you have left Peter?"

"If you'd asked me last Friday, straight after our wonderful encounter, I would probably have said yes, but now I'm not sure. It wasn't all going to happen at once. We were going to take time and get to know each other." Jennifer noticed the taxi pulling up outside. "Oh, Carol! I don't want to go to the funeral service."

"You could just go and keep your distance. Wait until they go into the church; go around the side of the church and then you can listen to the service through the window - or come back, phone me. I'm sure there must be a telephone box. Here's the number of the hotel. I won't go to the garden centre till you come back."

"Thank you, Carol." Jennifer kissed Carol on her cheek.

"Did he say green car?"

"Yes."

"Simon and I were Mr and Mrs Green."

Carol watched Jennifer get into the taxi and disappear down the road. She then ordered another cup of coffee from reception and returned to where they had been sitting earlier, in the corner by the fire. She sat down, picked up the local paper and flicked through, stopping at page five. She read the headline: 'Local man, Mr Richard Lawson, was killed on his way home from his London office'. Carol read it again. Simon wasn't dead! It was his brother! Oh, my goodness! She's going to the funeral. Oh, God! What can I do? She'll have the shock of her life! Why didn't Simon get in touch with her? Her coffee arrived, "Do you sell cigarettes?" she asked.

"Yes," replied the waitress.

"I don't usually smoke - in fact, I gave up years ago."

"You can have one of mine."

"Can I? Oh, thank you." The waitress offered her a cigarette and lit it for her.

"Thank you. I don't suppose it's possible to have a brandy, too?"

The waitress nodded. "Of course."

"I've had rather a shock."

The waitress walked off towards the bar.

That's given me such a shock! Poor Jennifer is going to get an even bigger one, thought Carol, as she shakily drew on her cigarette.

CHAPTER 28

Jennifer was in the back of the taxi, which was being driven by a local man.

"You going to the funeral?" he asked. Jennifer nodded. "The whole family is devastated about the accident. It happened last Friday night. He hit a cattle wagon that had broken down on a bend. The Lawson boys have always driven too fast... The funeral doesn't start until eleven-thirty."

"I know," replied Jennifer. "I'm meeting someone".

They arrived at the church a few minutes later and Jennifer paid the taxi driver. "Would you like me to come and pick you up afterwards? Here's my card. Just give me a ring from the telephone box over there." He pointed and smiled.

"Thank you very much. Goodbye." It was a green car! Oh, how she had enjoyed being Mrs Green. She stood there. What am I going to do for a whole hour? She spotted a pub opposite. I could go in there for a while, she thought. No, I feel like taking a walk. It's so strange, she thought, being here on my own. She could hear organ music coming from the little church – the organist practising funeral music. Music for Simon's funeral. Tears drizzled down her cheeks. She got her clean hanky out of her coat pocket and dabbed her face.

Jennifer walked towards the music. It was a warm, sunny day and she wandered down the path towards the church. A pretty building, thought Jennifer. The trees were laden with lovely cherry blossom. So lovely. She turned the corner and walked down the side of the church, where she spotted a bench. I'll sit here for a while, she thought, then I'll go and have a stiff drink. Perhaps I could watch the funeral cortège from the pub car park and then have another drink and phone Carol to pick me up. Yes, I'll do that, said Jennifer to herself, as she turned her face to the warm, comforting sun.

The vicar appeared out of a side door, accompanied by another man. Dash! At a time like this, why don't I wear glasses? Always too vain, aren't you, Jennifer? I think it might be Simon's brother. She was squinting and the sun was not helping, either.

"Thank you," she heard the man say. That sounded familiar, but different. I think I must need my hearing tested as well as my eyesight. Oh, he's coming this way! I'll turn around. Jennifer, you stupid girl. He doesn't even know you exist! You're just sitting in the sunshine. She looked at him as he approached her. He didn't have a twin, did he?

"Jenny, Jenny!" The man ran towards her.

"Simon, Simon, Simon!" Jennifer burst into tears as he sat down by her side.

"Why are you here?"

"I've come for your funeral!"

"Oh, no, my darling Jenny!"

"I phoned Monday morning, just as I promised, and was told that you were dead." She thumped his chest with both fists. "Dead, Simon. Dead. You were dead. Oh, I feel so sick. I feel as though I'm going to faint!" Simon put his arm around her. "I don't know how I've coped. I've had a terrible week."

Simon squeezed her closer to him. "Oh, my darling Jenny". He gave her the clean handkerchief from his pocket. "I'm so sorry that you've had to endure so much. You're in shock. Let's go to my car - it's just over there." He guided her off the bench. She was still crying and visibly shaking.

"When I phoned my office on Monday morning, my secretary gave me the message that Mrs Darling had phoned and that you had been told that it was my brother."

"Oh, Simon, I'm so sorry."

Simon opened the door of his car for Jennifer, then went around to the other side and got in. He started up the engine and set off. "I was hoping that you would phone again the Monday after the funeral, when I would be back in my office. It's been a lousy week. Richard's wife, Mary, had to be hospitalised. She's on very strong tranquilisers. I stepped in to organise the funeral and have been going over the details of the service with the vicar just now. I loved my brother. We were very good friends and I'm going to miss him so much. It all happened very quickly. After I said goodbye to you at the station, I went back to my office to try to shift one or two meetings around, so that I could come to see you the following week. I then left my office and bumped into a friend - Sam. He asked me if I was in a hurry and did I fancy a drink." Simon pulled over and stopped the car. They were on the outskirts of the village. "I've missed you," he said, as he took her in his arms and kissed her, reawakening in her all those feelings again.

"Oh, Simon! I love you so much."

"Oh, Jenny, my Jenny. How I have longed for us to be back together again." He kissed her tears away.

"Tell me more about what happened that Friday evening," said Jennifer, between wiping her eyes.

"So, Sam and I went for a drink. Then I got home about nine-thirty. I had approached my village from a different direction. If I had come this way, I would have known earlier. Ugh! It really upsets me. We were very close in business, as well as good friends... I could do with a drink."

"Me, too," agreed Jennifer,

"Where are you staying?" he asked.

"I have a room at the Red Lion... I was in such a state on Monday. Then, as soon as I put the phone down, having spoken to your receptionist, my friend, Carol, came over. Oh, Simon, I've relived everything we did. It's been like living in a dream – quite surreal and zombie-ish, really. Carol is waiting for me. She drove me here and has been wonderful. I've cried buckets and Peter just thought I was missing Lydia. I neglected Bess and Chi, had hundreds of baths, drank loads." She sighed. "I wanted to come here today to say goodbye and get on with my life."

"You're not going to say goodbye, though, are you?" he pleaded. "Can you stay tonight and I'll take you home tomorrow?"

"No, Simon, it's not fair on Carol. She wants to get back, as she has a sick mother."

"I'd like to meet this Carol. She sounds very nice, having looked after you so well."

"She's lovely. I told her how handsome you are."

"Oh, Jenny, you poor darling, with all those awful things going on in your mind." He stroked her hair. "I've done nothing but think of you all week. When I got back last Friday, Sylvia had already departed for a long weekend trip to France.

Since she returned on Monday, I've been sleeping in my dressing room."

"When did you hear about Richard?" asked Jennifer.

"Late on Friday evening. Mary's sister phoned me. I just couldn't believe it. I still can't."

"I didn't know that he lived in your village," said Jennifer.

"He doesn't. He lives near the Red Lion, where you stayed last night. In fact, I was at his house last night and I nearly popped into the pub for a drink on my way back home. I was with an old school pal of his, who's staying with us. We didn't go for a drink in the end because he wanted to go back to my home. Seeing Mary had upset him."

Jennifer suddenly looked at her watch. "Simon, the time! You must go!"

"I seem to have heard those words before," said Simon.

"The funeral!"

He nodded. "Yes. I'll take you back to your hotel." He started the car. "You won't change your mind about staying tonight?" He kissed her again, demonstrating that he had every intention of trying to persuade her to change her mind.

"No, Simon. However many times you kiss me - and how I have missed those lips! - the answer is still no." She smiled at him, as she gazed again into those wonderful eyes.

"Are you feeling a little better now?" he asked.

"No. I have a hell of a headache."

He leant forward and took a box of aspirin out of the glove compartment. "The least I can do," he said, offering it to Jennifer.

"Thank you. I'm still in shock at seeing you!"

Simon drove the car a little further and they pulled up outside the hotel. Simon got out and went around to Jennifer's side of the car. He opened her door and she climbed out. They were standing close to each other, each looking intently into the other's beloved face. "Will you phone?" asked Simon.

"Yes, I'll phone you on Monday morning." She smiled.

He kissed her tenderly on her cheek and then her lips. He held her tightly as she melted into his body. "I do love you, Mrs Jennifer Darling." He reluctantly let go of his hold of her and got back into his car. He wound down his window and smiled. Those legs, he thought to himself.

Those eyes, thought Jennifer. Love you. Go Simon! She blew him a kiss and he was gone.

to be continued...

Printed in Great Britain
by Amazon